CAPITAL GAMES

G.A. HAUSER

CAPITAL GAMES
Copyright © G.A. HAUSER, 2008
Cover art by Beverly Maxwell
ISBN Trade paperback: 978-1-60202-087-0
ISBN MS Reader (LIT): 978-1-60202-086-3
Other available formats (no ISBNs are assigned):
PDF, PRC & HTML

Linden Bay Romance, LLC
Palm Harbor, Florida 34684
www.lindenbayromance.com

First Linden Bay Romance publication: December 2007

I would like to say a special thank-you to my publisher and editors, Barbara Perfetti and Lori James. Where would I be without your faith and guidance? This one's for you.

Chapter One

"Who the hell is he?" he growled.

"Some new high flier ol' man Parsons found."

Steve ground his jaw as he stared at the sleek, well-dressed man who was standing in the office corridor shaking hands and smiling at his boss.

"Rumor has it he's in line to take over the Foist account," Kevin whispered quietly.

As Kevin gazed at the action in the hallway, Steve snarled, "I've been working for that account for the last three years… What the fuck is Parsons doing?"

Kevin laughed softly. "I don't know, Steve, but if I were you, I'd keep an eye on him."

As Kevin walked away, Steve glared at the shared smiles and warm gestures he was witnessing. A pat on the back, a touch to an arm, nods of their heads; it all seemed like an agreement was being reached between two parties and he wasn't pleased with the implications.

The moment he had a chance, Steve caught sight of his boss entering his office alone. Glancing down the hall first, Steve rapped the solid oak door and heard him shout "come in" from the other side. "Harold? Ya got a minute?"

"Sure, Steve, come in. Have a seat."

Eying the enormous office space, the plate glass

windows showing an expansive view of Los Angeles' smog and beyond to the suburban hills, Steve nudged out one of the supple leather chairs and sat down, opening the button of his suit jacket. "Uh, look, Harold…I've been with the company now for six years, right?"

Harold smiled, pressing his fingers together like two large spiders mating.

"I've done all right…I've pulled in some big names on my own, handled some of our most difficult clients…"

"What's your point, Steve?"

"Well…there're rumors going around the office…"

"You know better than to fall prey to office gossip."

"Do I?"

"I think working for the LAPD has made you suspicious of everyone." Mr. Parsons laughed softly, raising his eyebrows.

"Yeah, all right. Maybe. But, you know I've been working toward getting that Foist account for ages—"

"I haven't made any decisions on that yet."

"Fair enough, Harold, but, suddenly word is out that there's this new high flier nosing around—"

"His name is Mark Richfield. He's not 'nosing around', as you put it…I've invited him to spend some time here and get a feel for us and our clients."

"Why?"

"Really, Steve. I'm beginning to resent your attitude."

That shut him up. He knew how outspoken he was and his mouth had gotten him into trouble before. "With all due respect, Harold, I just would hope you would tell me if I wasn't working up to speed or—"

"Steve, don't take it personally. I've no complaints about your work."

Sensing he was pushing his luck, Steve stood up and buttoned his jacket again. "Right. Thanks for your time, Harold."

"No problem, Steve."

As he shut the office door behind him, he felt more

insecure about his position than before he went in. Loosening his tie, which was suddenly choking around his neck, he stepped into the lounge and found a clean mug to pour a cup of coffee into. Hearing a noise at the door behind him, two men joking together as they entered, made him spin around to look. Grinding his teeth, Steve found the "new guy" with another office team member, appearing very mutually jovial.

"Oh!" Charlie shouted when he spotted him. "Steviebaby! Have you met Mark yet?"

Under his breath Steve muttered, "No." He couldn't even force a smile. When Mark's emerald green gaze reached his, Steve felt some incredible charismatic power and intelligence radiating from them that intimidated him instantly.

Charlie escorted Mark across the room, a hand on his low back as if he were pushing two opposing magnetic poles to meet. With something akin to a wicked smirk, Mark extended his hand.

"Mark Richfield, this is one of our top guns, Steve Miller. He's ex-LAPD so don't cross him. He's liable to shoot you!"

With a wry smile on his lips, Mark whispered sensuously, "I'll be sure to keep him in my sight."

Detecting a slight accent, Steve reluctantly accepted that hand and asked, "You British?"

"Aye. An ex-cop, eh? What brings you into the world of advertising?"

"Got sick of always watching my back."

"Then you are in the wrong business once more," Mark whispered impishly.

At that inflammatory remark, Steve broke off the handshake and stuffed his hand inside his pocket. "How long are you staying?"

"You mean in the country or in the company?" Mark's eyes gleamed wickedly.

"Both." Steve just noticed Charlie's amused expression.

"I've permanent leave to remain here in the States, but as far as here at Parsons & Co. I just don't know."

Gazing at that suspiciously knowing expression, Steve was certain Mark was hungry for that coveted position. Who wouldn't want to get their hands on a multi-million dollar account and a promotion? He turned his back on them, using the premise of reaching for his coffee cup, but in reality, he had nothing to say. Or should he clarify that as, nothing *nice* to say.

As if sensing the cold shoulder, Mark said softly to Charlie, "Thanks for the tour, mate. I've got some things to tend. Ta."

Peering over his shoulder, Steve caught Mark's mischievous smile before he vanished, then Charlie's equally wicked grin. "What?" Steve asked in annoyance after Mark had left the room. Did everyone know this new guy was after his job?

"You believe Parsons is even interested in him?"

"Why?" Steve stirred the milk into his black coffee.

"Well, he's a bit out of character for this place, you know—the long hair, the eccentric British air…"

"Yeah, whatever…" Steve sipped the hot brew, then headed to the door. Before he left to go to his office, Charlie shouted, "You see the memo on the Team Building Retreat?"

Stopping, turning around to face him, Steve replied, "No. What Team Building Retreat?"

"In New Mexico. All the execs have to go. Parsons says we need to work more as a team and less as adversaries."

"Are you joking?"

"No, I wish I was. No, Steve, I'm not joking. You want me to find the memo? You should have one in your box."

"No. I'll look through my paperwork. There is a pile I haven't had the time to sort through."

"Okay. See ya later."

Steve nodded and then carried his hot cup of coffee to his private office. He set the mug down, then leafed through some piles of loose notes. Picking one up, he read the title, 'Round-up Retreat! To all middle management and associate executives: *mandatory attendance* - Team Building and Leadership seminars'.

With his mouth hanging open in disbelief, Steve sighed, "Oh, my fricken' god. You have to be kidding me."

Coming through the door of his home, pulling off his tie as he stepped into his living room, Steve immediately went to the refrigerator for a beer. Stuffing the tie inside his jacket pocket, he draped the jacket over a chair and found a bottle opener. Cracking the beer open, he stood in the middle of the kitchen and drank it down, then wiped his mouth with the back of his hand and noticed his message light on his telephone machine flashing. He hit the button and heard his sister's voice. "Hello, Stevie...what's new? Barry and I wondered if you wanted to come over for dinner and visit with Chloe. Call me." He erased it, then lifted the phone.

"Hello?"

"Hi, Laura."

"Hey! Did you get my message?"

"Yes. I just got it now."

"You want to come by? Or do you already have plans?"

He sat down on one of the high stools near the breakfast counter, and set the bottle down so he could rub his exhausted face. "I don't know. What were you guys doing?"

"You sound funny. What happened?"

"Nothing...crap...I don't know."

"Come on, Steve. You can tell me anything. You know that. You missing LAPD?" she laughed.

"Ha...well, no, but believe me, sometimes I think this advertising business is more dangerous than being on the streets in LA. At least there I could justify shooting someone."

"Whoa! What the hell's going on over at Parsons &

Company?"

"I hear Chloe in the background...you have a minute?"

"Yeah, she's with Barry. Come on, Steve, it can't be any worse than losing Sonja. And you got over that."

"Ouch. You really know how to hurt a guy." He picked up his beer and sipped it again.

"Sorry. I didn't mean it that way."

"I know, it's all right...well, there's this account I've been really striving for at work. The guy who handles it is retiring shortly, and someone has to take over the account. Laura, it's big. I can't tell you how much money is in it."

"Really?"

"Yes. I'd kill for it....so, I've been working my ass off for the last three years, slaving, taking the crap accounts no one wants, working them into big money accounts, you know...getting the cash through the door."

"And?"

"Well, this new guy shows up today...some fricken' English guy, all flashy and bold, and rumor has it the account has his name on it. I just don't think its fair, Laura. I've been there, sweating, breaking my damn back for years for that account. Why the hell should some moron just waltz in and take it from me?"

"I think you should talk to your boss."

"I did." Steve finished the beer and set the bottle down again.

"And?"

"Well, he just about told me to keep my nose out."

"Shit!"

"Yeah, exactly. Christ, Laura, I'm so fucking furious."

"Well, you don't know for sure he's giving it to this English guy. You said it's just rumor."

"He'll get it. I can just tell. He's really got this aura of charm about him. I can't compete with that."

"Bull shit! Steve you are gorgeous, charming, and extremely bright. Don't sell yourself short. You clawed and scratched from the bottom of that company to third from the top! Stop belittling yourself and give yourself some credit."

"I'm not, Laura, but I'm telling ya, he's going to get it, and it's going to kill me."

"When are they making the decision?"

"I'm not sure. Roland hasn't left yet. But I assume they'll overlap us a little, you know, to get Roland to introduce whoever is getting it to the account and work with him a little first."

"Well, in the meantime, I suggest you just work hard and don't show how much this is bothering you. Parsons may be watching to see if you'll break under the pressure."

Rubbing his face again, Steve nodded his head, "Yes...yes, you're right."

"Now, are you coming over for dinner?"

"Yeah. Let me just get changed. I'll be by within the hour."

"Good. See you soon."

He hung up and stared into space. "You son of a bitch...you will not take that account from me, Richfield. Over my dead body."

Chapter Two

First thing in the morning Steve parked his Mercedes in his reserved space and locked it up. Briefcase in hand, he looked back at it as he went, admiring its sleek lines when a dark TVR pulled in next to it. He stopped short and investigated the unusual sports-car curiously. "Oh, you have to be kidding," he mumbled, when a very tall male with long dark hair emerged from it. Unable to resist, Steve waited until Mark noticed him, then stood still as that smirk of superiority made its way over.

"Officer Miller," Mark greeted him teasingly.

"I'm not a cop anymore." Steve resumed his walk to the elevators. "Since when did you get an executive parking spot? Does that mean you are already on the payroll?"

Mark watched as Steve pushed the button to go up, then replied, "And the key to the executive loo. How lucky can a bloke get?"

A few other office workers entered the elevator with them. Steve closed his mouth and pushed the number for the top floor, then felt Mark staring at him. He glanced up and caught that impish grin, then shook his head at Mark in annoyance. As the tiny box emptied out and only the two of them were left to ascend to the top floor, Mark said, "It doesn't look good, you know…"

"What doesn't?" Steve tried not to bite his head off.

"Your constant frown. Anyone would think your

knickers were wound too tight."

"Shut the fuck up."

"Oooh! They are wound up around your bollocks a bit, aren't they?" Mark taunted.

As Steve was about to shout something rude in reply the doors opened to their floor. Immediately Steve could see several co-workers in the area. Seeing Mark waiting for that come-back with so many witnesses present, Steve tightened his lips and headed to his office, the caustic reply rebounding throughout his temples.

Coming through his door, throwing his briefcase down, Steve had to take a moment to calm down before he could function.

"Mr. Miller? ...Steve?"

"Hmmm?" He turned around to see his secretary. "Oh...Mary, what is it?"

"Mr. Parsons wants the applications for the retreat on his desk this morning."

"Oh...I've got that paperwork here somewhere." He took off his jacket and hung it on the back of his door as she waited. Then trying not to show her his foul mood, he thumbed through the loose paperwork and then held up the form. "I haven't filled it out yet."

"Can I help you with it?"

"Sure." He handed it to her and then sat behind his desk as she took a seat in front of it and produced a pen.

"Right..." she began. "Name, address...that I can do...oh, it asks if you have any type of meal preference. Like if you are a vegetarian or something."

"No. I'm not." Steve tried to imagine this horrible retreat without cringing.

"Right...no medical conditions? No...uh, allergies? No. Emergency contact numbers?"

"Just use my mom's." He rattled it off to her and she nodded.

"That's it! I'll get this to Mr. Parsons for you."

"Thanks, Mary."

"Would you like me to get you a cup of coffee?"

"Yes. No rush." He smiled back at her as she left, then picked up the phone and started to get busy with his work.

A few hours later he visited the men's room. Standing at the urinal he heard someone enter behind him and then rolled his eyes as Mark stood at the urinal next to him. "Christ, can't I do anything without you around?"

After unzipping his trousers, Mark glanced down at Steve first, then replied, "You can't compete with me in any way, can you, Officer Miller?"

Finishing up, deliberately not taking the bait, fastening his pants with annoyance, Steve walked to the sink and washed his hands, then checked his hair in the mirror.

Within a moment, Mark was doing the same. "They don't let you grow your hair long in the police, do they?"

Drying his hands on a towel, Steve replied, "I wouldn't grow it like yours anyway. You look like a little frilly girl from the back."

"Not from the front though, where it counts." Mark winked at him, pushing his hips forward in a sexual tease.

Catching the gesture, Steve crossed his arms over his chest and stood tall. "What the hell is your problem? What the fuck do you want with this company anyway? Aren't there companies back in the UK you could haunt?"

"Yes, perhaps…but, I like everything bigger and better. Isn't that what it's like here in the US? They say everything is better here."

Another man entered the bathroom. Before Steve could once again be caught being hostile to this newcomer and accused of foul play, he left the room.

Not looking over his shoulder to see if he was being shadowed, Steve was about to grab his coat and briefcase to go meet a client when Mr. Parsons stopped him in the hall. "I want you to help with one of the presentations at the retreat, Steve."

Distracted by the earlier incident in the men's room, Steve nodded, "Yes, all right."

"With your background and experience with the force, I want you to help with one of the team building exercises."

"Yes...okay, Harold. Anything."

"You on your way out?"

"Yes. I've a meeting with P & M."

"Oh! Great! Get them on board here, Steve. They're a huge account."

"I'll try my best, sir." Steve nodded, then slipped out, grumbling under his breath, "...and so was Kippers, and Hark and Company..." He breathed out in anger, "What more do you want, you SOB? My fucking blood?"

A signed contract in his briefcase, Steve stopped off at a café and ordered a latte and sandwich. When he was settled down at a table by the window, he flipped out his mobile phone and dialed. "Mary...it's me. Can you transfer me to Parsons' secretary? I tried his line directly but it was busy...thanks." He waited while he was connected to Mr. Parson's secretary, then said, "Ray? It's Steve. Is the big boss in? Good. Thanks." He sipped the coffee and stared at his sandwich as his stomach grumbled. "Harold?"

"Steve!"

"I've got a signed contract for five years in my briefcase."

"Well done! That's fantastic...really. A job very well done."

"Thanks, sir. I'm just grabbing a bite and then I'll get it on your desk."

"Very good! I'm looking forward to it. Enjoy your lunch."

"Thanks. See you soon." He hung up and then whispered, "Take that, you long-haired limey."

When he returned to his office there was a buzz in the air. Smiling, he wondered if everyone got the news of his new account. In anticipation of pats on the back and handshakes, he looked around the halls and offices at the hive of activity. Feeling a little odd when no one seemed to acknowledge his victory, Steve set his briefcase down on his desk and removed the signed contract from it, then with his head held high he knocked on Mr. Parson's door. A shout bid him entry. When he found Mark there, a glass of champagne in his hand and a big cheesy grin on his face, Steve's smile dropped.

"Come in, Steve! Come in!" Harold waved him to enter as if he were a circus leader in the middle of three rings.

"I have the contract from P & M..." Steve felt disoriented by Mark's strange smile.

"Oh, yes, right. Just set that down. Grab a glass, Steve! Richfield here has just signed us a contract with the BBC!"

Staggered by the news, Steve suddenly felt as if his puny little multimillion dollar contract was meaningless. As Mr. Parsons poured another glass of "the bubbly", Steve felt almost paralyzed by Mark's unnerving grin. The glass shoved into his numb hand, Mr. Parsons toasting their newest account and employee, Steve felt as if he was squeezing the glass so tightly that it would shatter in his palm. The amount of rage and jealousy he was enduring felt like physical blows. It suddenly occurred to him he was not equipped for this battle. Staring at that unbelievable charming grin, those sparkling green eyes, that ridiculously long hair and that chiseled jaw, for the first time since he met him, Steve felt completely inferior to him and the anger in him grew.

Seemingly loving the moment, Mark tapped Steve's glass and whispered, "To me," then sipped the expensive champagne while his stare was riveted to Steve's.

Someplace in the background, Mr. Parsons was praising his two favorite executives, shouting out chants and hurrahs like a cheerleader. But Steve heard none of it. As if he had tunnel vision, his fury and frustration were aimed at this one man. One who was enjoying his victory like the fine glass of champagne he was savoring.

Once home, Steve changed into his running clothes and tied the house key to his sneaker. Pounding the pavement, he ran his frustration off and tried not to think of the dreadful afternoon and that smug expression on Mark's face.

The sweat soon dripping down his skin in the heat of summer in LA, Steve wiped at the droplets as they ran down his temples and rough jaw. "Fucking moron...fucking-mother-fucking-moron..." he hissed as he clenched his fists, his feet gaining speed as he hit a decline in the pavement. "How do I compete with that? How? Christ, I feel like strangling him. I can't stand it... Christ, he'll get that Foist account... BBC? How can I get an account that big? The BBC? For Christ's sake!" He heard a car horn and whipped his head around to someone flipping him off as he almost forgot to stop at the curb near a cross street. He regained his composure and renewed his pace again passing a park with children feeding ducks. "I'll be humiliated. I'll have to quit. I can't have him lording it over me. I can't." Remembering the hierarchy of the police, Steve didn't need someone he despised looking down at him ever again. "There must be another big firm in LA...I'll have to start looking." But he knew he was already with the biggest advertising agency in the state. He'd never get the same pay elsewhere.

As the heat and miles began to take their toll, Steve looped back to his home, barely looking at the scenery or enjoying the summer's day. Back at his home once again, he untied his shoelace and impaled the door with the key, then reveled in the air-conditioned coolness and headed to the kitchen for a bottle of cold water. Checking the time as he sucked it down, he found it was after seven p.m., and still very warm out. Finishing the bottle of water quickly, he exited the house to his garage, and in the cool shade of its interior he punched a punching bag, imagining it was Richfield's head.

Chapter Three

Saturday morning, he packed a suitcase that was spread open on his bed. Throwing clothing into it in frustration, he was thinking that even the idea of spending time with his co-workers at this retreat was enough to bring his blood pressure to the boil. "This is the last thing I need," he muttered. "Stupid fricken, retreat...I hate this shit. I'd rather go to boot camp than this!" He flapped the suitcase shut, then latched it. Standing in his bedroom, wondering what clothing he could possibly need at this farcical escapade, he shrugged his shoulders as if it didn't make a difference anyway. "I'll be quitting after they appoint that asshole to the position."

Taking his keys, his mobile phone and charger, and his briefcase, Steve secured his home and set the alarm. Loading up his car, he found the directions and read them again. "Interstate 40, right." He tossed the instructions and map down on the passenger seat, then rolled back the convertible roof. "If they thought I was going to sit on a bus and sing camp songs, they are completely insane," he scoffed to himself. Blasting rock and roll music, Steve made for the highway and tried to clear his mind of the anger for a few hours. How bad could this retreat be? He knew the employees better than Richfield did. How bad could it be?

Eight hours of highway behind him, Steve pulled into a long dusty drive and passed under a cliché painted wooden ranch sign. "Oh, Christ," he grimaced at the Hollywood look of the place. Images of rodeos and campfires flashed through his mind in horror. "Why, why, why…" he moaned helplessly.

Parking his car near a chartered bus and a few pick-up trucks, Steve shut the engine and stared at a single floor structure with a sign that read, "Register here, partner" over the door in black paint. When he entered the lobby he found it already filled with his co-workers laughing and shouting in excited tones as if they were children at summer camp. Charlie spotted him first and waved him over. "Miller! You missed all the fun!"

"Oh?" Steve caught a few curious eyes as he made his way across the lobby and its uneven wood flooring.

"Yeah! Richfield had us all singing some raunchy pub song on the bus on the ride here. Why did you drive? Christ, it's a long haul on your own."

"Uh…" before he answered him, he raised his jaw to see those green eyes watching him.

A hand touched his back. When Steve looked over his shoulder, Mr. Parsons was there. "You missed all the fun, Steve," he echoed Charlie's words. "It wasn't very team-oriented of you to come on your own."

Sensing his first faux pas, Steve tried to look away from that unnerving stare to come up with a plausible lie. "I had a last minute detail to take care of. Sorry. I just couldn't get to the office in time to catch the bus. My sister phoned and said my niece was ill. Otherwise you know I would have been there."

"Oh, sorry to hear that," Mr. Parsons said. "Nothing serious, I hope?"

"No…no, actually, she was alarmed for no reason at all. She's fine." He smiled his best smile, nodding his head, then turned to see that intense stare once more as Mr.

15

Parsons left him to chat with another employee. Giving the Brit a dirty look in return, Steve distracted himself by listening to some joke Kevin had heard earlier on the bus that he had missed.

Once they were all given a room assignment and itinerary, the group disbanded temporarily to get their belongings put away. When Steve checked his room number and carried his bag with him to the correct wing, he opened the door to see four single beds in dismay. "Crap."

Behind him, Charlie and Kevin shoved at him to get out of their way as they stumbled in and had a look around. "Four to a room?" Kevin laughed, "Christ, this is too funny."

Images of finding a nice hotel down the road for some privacy passed through Steve's weary mind.

The two men quickly claimed half the beds in the room, then had a look at the bathroom facilities to ensure they did indeed have one attached and not somewhere down the hall. As Charlie read out the next mornings' events from a flier, Steve heard the door opening. Seeing Mark poke his head in made his heart sink. "Please don't tell me you're in here as well."

As if checking his paperwork once again, Mark looked at the number on the door, then grinned wickedly. "Hullo roomie," he purred.

Rubbing his eyes in agony, Steve mumbled, "Can this get any worse?"

The other two men weren't nearly as upset as they jumped up and gave Mark a high-five in excitement. "All right! Party!" Kevin shouted like a juvenile delinquent.

As Steve watched, Mark walked to the last unclaimed bed and set his case on it. Once he had, he looked over at the one next to him and asked, "Yours?" to Steve.

"Unfortunately," Steve replied.

"I don't snore, I assure you," Mark quipped, then flicked his hair back from his face as the warmth of the room began to get to him. "It's so flamin' hot here. I'm not used to it."

Charlie sat up on the bed and asked, "Is it cold in London?"

"Yes! Compared to this, it's the polar ice caps."

About to make a comment about how if Mark couldn't take the heat then he should get out of New Mexico, Steve stopped as the man pulled his t-shirt over his head revealing a very spectacular physique. After Mark wiped his face with the material and tossed it on the bed, he met Steve's eyes again. "Am I exciting the cop?"

"Oh, fuck you, you conceited bastard," Steve growled. The two other men snickered in amusement.

"Oh, this should be fun," Charlie replied. "The two big cats cooped up in the same cage! Meow!"

Having had enough of them already, Steve left the room, not looking back. Dying for a beer, he tried to sniff out a bar or employee who could point him to one. Before he made it across the lobby's wide oak floor, Mr. Parsons was shouting his name and dragging a heavy-set woman with black rimmed glasses with him. "Miller! Miller! This is Petula...she's organizing the events and I told her you are to help with the physical part of the team building exercise."

"Huh? Help with what?" Steve was gripped on his arm by her, as if she were latching on and not letting him go.

"I'll leave you to it." Mr. Parsons waved as he fled.

"He told me you were once a cop." Petula grinned at him. "Good! You can pretend you're directing traffic!"

"Huh?" Steve tried to dig his heels in as she dragged him across the lobby.

"I've got some charts and graphs for you to look at, but I think you should be the one to detail the actual project."

"Project? What project?" He looked behind him for an escape, but no trap door existed.

By midnight he scuffed his weary feet back to his room. Numbers, exercises, catch phrases, all spinning in his head, he tried to be quiet as he used his key and unlatched the door. Deep breathing and snoring greeted his ears. Tiptoeing to his bed, Steve stripped down to his jockey shorts and then peeled back the light bedspread with the horseshoe and pony print on it. Just before he closed his eyes he found a set of green ones staring at him. Rolling over, giving him his back, he shut his eyes and fell into a deep slumber.

Chapter Four

Once the breakfast of sausages and scrambled eggs had been devoured in a wagon train-style environment, Steve, dressed in shorts in anticipation of the hot day, headed wearily to their first lecture of the three-day event: Salesmanship and Communication. And he thought LAPD was bad? Wincing in agony at the idea of sitting in a stuffy room having to roll-play and listen to long-winded speeches with pie-charts for examples, Steve imagined giving his notice and getting the hell out of Dodge.

The chairs were set up in a circle with an easel holding a large pad breaking the circumference. "Oh, Christ, just shoot me..." He found a seat on the opposite side of his nemesis, and picked up some paperwork from the chair before he sat on it. A rough outline of the morning itinerary was printed on it. Making a sound in his throat of disgust at the agenda, he rubbed his unshaven jaw tiredly and wished the entire event could conclude and he could be cut free.

"Hello, partners!" a strange looking man in a cowboy hat shouted to get everyone seated and quiet. "Let's mosey on into our chairs and get started."

"Mosey?" Steve repeated sarcastically, then heard the woman next to him snicker in agreement at his comment. After an hour of what Steve considered "pure bullshit", they were given a break and then returned to their seats. Soon after, the man shouted, "Let's all form groups! Count to three and go around the room."

Watching as his co-workers sounded off, he said "One" as his turn came and then they were instructed, "Number one's in front, two's in back, and three's to the left". Grabbing the back of his chair in one hand and the paperwork in the other, Steve couldn't hide his frown as he moved to the front. Once he sat down in the seat, he looked up and then moaned, "Oh, crap."

"Hello, roomie." Mark smiled, setting his chair next to Steve's.

Raising his hand high, Steve shouted to no one in particular, "Can I change groups?" but he was ignored in the noise of the room.

"Oh, don't be a spoil sport. That is what you Yanks say, right? Spoil sport?" Mark asked someone else in the group.

"You're like the plague." Steve rolled the papers up like a tube, tighter and tighter until they were as narrow as a straw.

Mark replied, "A little nervous, Officer Miller?" and nodded his head to the paperwork.

"Why do you keep calling me that?" Steve demanded. "You see a badge anywhere on me? A uniform? A fucking gun?"

"I don't know? Is that a gun in your pocket?" Mark whispered in a hiss.

Before Steve could reply, someone was handing out a role playing scenario. "Okay, partners! Decide who will be the client, and who will be the salesman!"

The two men with Mark and Steve seemed to shrink away at the thought of participating. Seeing their body language, Steve cringed as Mark decided to delegate. "You sell me, Officer Miller."

"Who died and made you boss?" Steve shook his head at the absurdity.

"Parsons doesn't have to die," Mark replied, clicking his tongue wickedly.

"Oh screw you!"

The facilitator approached their group. "Who's who?"

Bret and David quickly pointed Steve and Mark out.

"You sell this Eskimo a refrigerator in Alaska." Steve was handed a paper with some specs on appliances on it.

After the man left, Mark stuck his tongue into his cheek and stared at Steve. "Okay, Miller. Sell me. Show me how good you are."

About to wipe the smirk off his face with a fist to the jaw, Steve stopped himself from actually swinging and making contact when Mr. Parsons stood behind their tiny circle. "Who's the salesman?" he asked excitedly.

Three fingers pointed to Steve.

"Great! What are you selling?"

"A refrigerator, to him." Steve couldn't even force a smile.

"Oh?" Mr. Parsons appeared very amused.

"I'm an Eskimo," Mark chuckled happily.

"Fucking brown-noser," Steve muttered out of the side of his mouth.

"Really? A refrigerator to an Eskimo. That sounds like quite a challenge." Mr. Parsons stood back, folding his arms over his chest. "Go ahead, Steve. Give it the hard sell."

Hating it, every minute of it, Steve read over the product specifications quickly, then finally looked at Mark's completely patronizing grin. "Uh, hello, sir, do you mind if—"

"Stop." Mark held up his hand.

"Stop? Why?"

"You didn't even knock on my door."

"Knock on your—?"

"That's right, Steve," Mr. Parsons agreed, "Knock first."

Biting his tongue on speaking his mind at this absurdity, Steve pretended to knock, saying, "Knock, knock."

"Who is it?" Mark sang sweetly.

"It's the refrigerator salesman."

"Who?"

"The refrigerator salesman!" Steve shouted.

"I didn't call any refrigerator salesman," Mark taunted.

"Look, can I just talk to you for a minute about—"

"Why would I need a refrigerator when my entire back garden is frozen? I'm afraid you're wasting your time, Mr. Salesman."

Glancing at Mr. Parsons' face as he waited to see how he would get the door open in this situation, Steve cleared his throat and said, "But, I have a free gift."

"Oh?" Mark feigned interest.

"Yes. If you open the door and let me tell you about our fantastic new product, I'll give you a free gift."

Mark pretended to open the door. "Where's my gift?" He held out his hand.

"I would like to tell you about this incredible new appliance first. It won't freeze everything, like your cold backyard. You won't have to thaw your milk and eggs on the fire anymore."

"Oh?" Mark batted his lashes, trying to distract him.

Slightly put off, Steve forced himself to concentrate. "Yes…you know how annoying it is…sticking everything on the stove just to thaw it…well, with this new refrigerator you won't have to anymore. I guarantee you will be satisfied."

"You want to satisfy me? Is that my free gift?" Mark puckered his lips and made kissing noises.

Steve tried not to be distracted by the laughing of the other three observers. Restraining the urge to pull back and pretend to punch him in the "kisser", Steve continued, "Uh, the appliance comes with a full warranty and money back if you're not fully satisfied."

"Oh, I'll be satisfied, love…"

Throwing up his hands, Steve shouted, "I can't do this if he's acting like that!"

"Why not?" Mr. Parsons prodded. "Keep going. You haven't closed the sale yet."

Shifting in his chair, Steve looked back at that condescending smirk and tried to stare him down. Once again he cleared his throat, and then said, "Let me just bring the refrigerator inside your house...er...igloo, and you can try it out. If for any reason you feel it isn't living up to your standards, give me a call and I'll come get it. No worries or obligations."

"Yes, why don't you stick it inside? I'm sure you're up to my standards, love."

Resisting the urge to once again throw up his hands in exasperation at the double-entendre, Steve persevered. "Good. I'll get my men to install it for you. Thank you for your business."

Smiling demonically, Mark extended his hand to seal the deal. Reluctantly, Steve took it. The grip was strangling and wouldn't release.

"Well done, boys!" Mr. Parsons clapped. "Very entertaining."

Steve wrenched out of the death grip and tried to smile at his boss without sneering.

The facilitator shouted "time", and they all waited for the next scenario. Feeling that British stare on his profile, Steve glanced over and found that sly grin. Trying not to hate him, he ran his hand back through his hair and pretended he was listening to the man in front of the room.

"My turn to sell you..." Mark winked at Steve.

Steve gestured to the other two men in frustration. "What about David and Bret? Why the hell is it my turn again?"

Bret shook his head in fear. "Not me! You two are doing just fine. I hate these things. I get stage fright."

The facilitator handed another scenario out to the three groups. Mark quickly snatched it to read. "Oh, yes," he chuckled.

"What now?" Steve groaned, rubbing his face in agony.

"I'm the devil and I have to sell you a new soul."

"Sell me a soul?" Steve asked, "Don't you mean buy it?"

Mark flipped the paper around so Steve could read it. "It says sell, love, not buy. I suppose you already sold it to me and now need a replacement."

"Begin!" was shouted at them.

Steve crossed his arms and slouched in his seat as he waited for this "magnificent" salesman to perform.

Mark pulled his chair up so his bare legs were against Steve's. Steve peered down at the contact quickly, then back at Mark's demonic eyes.

Beginning his roll-play, Mark leaned forward, close to Steve's face and whispered, "I can tell you aren't whole."

"What?" Steve tilted his head in disbelief.

"There's a hole in you, love. A place where you have a need. One only needs to look and they can see you are a very unhappy man."

"Shut up."

Mark gestured to the other two men to sympathize, as if the comment had made his point. "Look, mate…"

Steve peered down as Mark's hand rested on his exposed thigh, then back into those mesmerizing eyes again.

"I'm here to heal you…make you whole and happy once more. All you need to do is allow me. It won't take long. Just a tiny minute of your time."

A wash of chills rushed up Steve's spine. This Brit was leaning so close to his face it was as if they could press their lips together. The room vanished around him, the sounds melded to a murmur, and all that he could see were two emerald green irises and rose-colored lips.

"Trust me," Mark purred, then ran his hand over the hair on Steve's leg gently. "Trust me to give you what you need. Will you do that, love?"

As if he suddenly realized they were not alone and were being watched by at least two very interested males in their group and even possibly their boss, Steve jolted back and moved Mark's hand off his thigh. "What the hell is going on here?"

"Time!"

Steve felt he had to literally shake off the hypnotic trance. He moved his chair back, making more space between them and looked at Bret and David to see their reactions. They were grinning wickedly at him as if Mark had indeed sold him that new soul he was lacking.

A minute later they adjourned to take a break to get coffee or go to the restroom. Standing up to stretch his legs, Steve walked to one of the windows to see the blazing sun outdoors. As he felt the heat of someone behind him he looked over his shoulder. Seeing it was Mark, he said, "Anyone could use sex to sell. It's the oldest trick in the book."

"Then why don't you use it?"

"Firstly because it's not my style and secondly, it can get you into trouble."

"Don't you like a bit of trouble, Officer Miller?"

Leaning back against the window, Steve met that unnerving smile and said, "Are you coming on to me?"

"No. Do you want me to?"

"No!"

"One thing we agree on then."

"Good." Steve looked around the room to see if anyone was listening, then he hissed, "You won't get the Foist account."

"Won't I?"

"No."

"We'll see." Mark narrowed his eyes at him.

"What will you do? Suck Parsons' cock for it?" Steve sneered.

That took Mark back. "Do what?"

Instantly Steve felt guilty. "Look, I didn't mean—"

"Okay, back into your groups!"

That playful smirk had changed to deep insult and anger. Steve felt like crap for it and wished he could retract that statement. But it had vanished in the air, like poisonous mist.

The rest of the seminar both he and Mark sat mute as David and Bret did the next two scenarios. When they broke for lunch Steve found Mark leaving the room quickly, slipping away.

"Shit..." Steve imagined chasing after him to apologize, then just shrugged to himself at the futility.

A banquet of barbequed beef and corn on the cob was set out for them on large picnic tables covered with tablecloths of red and white checkerboard squares. The chefs all had cowboy hats on and bandanas around their necks in the heat. Steve sat next to Charlie who was already slopping down some spareribs. "Is there any beer?" Steve asked desperately. "I'm gasping."

With brown sticky sauce over his lips, Charlie shook his head, "No, man...no booze. Kevin and I want to make a beer run but we don't have a car...wait—you do."

"I do. And I think there was a truck stop a few miles back." Steve searched the area for Mr. Parsons. "I don't know how we can do it now."

"Wait till dark...after the day's events. We can have a few in our room before we sleep."

Watching Charlie renew his zealous slurping of the ribs, Steve thought of Mark in that room and endured a wave of guilt as it passed over him. Looking up from his plate, he noticed Mark give his table a glance, then appear to move on. Kevin stopped him and pointed to the table where they were sitting. As Steve watched carefully, it appeared Mark was very pained to join him at present. Without meeting his eyes, Mark sat down with his plate and attempted to neatly eat food that could not be handled with care.

Kevin laughed at him and said, "Dig in, Richfield. There's no way to do it daintily."

Steve caught a quick glimpse from those verdant eyes, then Mark replied, "Bullocks," under his breath and picked up the corn to gnaw off the cob.

"You all right?" Charlie asked him.

Steve's stomach tightened as he waited for Mark's reply.

Again Mark's eyes darted to Steve's. "Not too pleased with the present company."

"Ohhh?" Charlie grinned in delight. "The two big cats at

it again?"

"Shut up," Steve snarled.

"I love it," Charlie gloated, licking his sauce-covered fingers. "Can't wait for more team building exercises!"

"I said shut up!" Steve roared, then caught Kevin and Mark glaring at him. When someone tapped him on the shoulder from behind, Steve almost bit their head off. Seeing it was Petula, he sighed and tried to smile. "Oh. Hi."

"We're up next. You done eating?"

Looking back at his barely touched plate, Steve stood up and nodded. He tossed the food into the garbage and followed her. When he looked back, Mark's furious eyes were following him.

"Here's the area I was talking about last night. You see? The fence is down. So, you need to organize teams to fix it. Like I said, I would divide the group into two or three, then have someone chop, someone dig, and the rest assemble."

Nodding, losing interest completely, wondering why he was selected for this job, Steve wiped the trickle of sweat off his face and brushed a fly from his naked knee.

"There are the logs. There are axes, and there're the hammers, shovels, and spikes."

Nodding, looking at things without really seeing them, Steve put his hands on his hips and tried to feign interest.

"They have two hours to complete it. So there is a time limit."

"Right. Okay."

"The team that wins gets a treat."

Pausing, looking back at her, he asked, "Team that wins?"

"Yes."

As if he were lost suddenly, he shook his head to clear it and asked, "Wait, they're in competition?"

A look of exasperation on her face, she said, "Did you listen to anything I said last night?"

"I thought I had."

"Look, Mr. Miller, you split the group into two or three,

each team has to assemble their part of the fence…hence the team building. It makes them work together. Your job is to keep them going, shout encouragement, and straighten them out if they stray."

"Okay, okay…" He held up his hand as if to say 'enough'.

When she walked away he could hear her mumbling, "Why the heck they picked this guy for this job is beyond me…"

Within a few minutes he could see the crowd making its way over to him. The boiling sun was almost directly overhead. Mr. Parsons and one of the facilitators were standing in the rear to observe. Steve cleared his throat and shouted to quiet everyone.

"Okay, people! Look, count off one and two!" After they had he pointed, shouting, "One's here! Two's here!" He watched Mark and Charlie move to the left with six others, as another group of eight moved to the right. Appearing defensive and angry, Mark's arms were in a tight knot over his chest. His shorts were high on his thighs, and his t-shirt taut on his chest.

"Your job, as a team, is to repair this fence. Group one has this area, and group two that area." He made sure it was clear. "Delegate one person to chop, one to hammer, one to dig, one to hold…you get the idea. You are being timed. So, don't spend too much time deciding. Winner gets a prize. Ready?" Steve checked his watch, then waved his hand like he was starting a race.

Watching the chaos that ensued, he shook his head in disbelief. Marching to group one, he found them all arguing over who would get the hard part, chopping. "What the hell's going on?" Steve asked.

"It's too fucking hot to chop wood! Are you kidding?" Charlie shouted.

"Give me the fucking thing!" Steve grabbed an axe and set the wood up. A mark had already been made on the log. He hacked at it as the others stood and watched. When he had made the end taper to a point he wiped his face and shouted, "Get on with digging the post!" as if they were complete idiots, then he walked to the next group.

"Wanker," Mark murmured under his breath.

Steve heard it and twisted around, just missing his sneering stare.

It was as if he were leading two bands of imbeciles. No one wanted to work in the mid-day sun. With his skills as a leader in the spotlight, Steve felt he had no choice but to lead by example, but it was exhausting work. After doing the same for group two, he walked back to see group one's progress. "Is this a joke?"

"What?" David had the shovel in his hand but was doing nothing with it.

"You still haven't dug a hole?" Steve gestured to the ground.

"It's hard work!"

Snatching the shovel from his hand, Steve dug through the sandy dirt, then stuffed the pole into the ground. Next he swung a heavy sledge hammer down on it and it penetrated instantly into the dry dirt. He handed the shovel back to David and said, "Do the next one."

"Geezuz," David replied sarcastically, "not everyone is Mr. Muscle!"

Checking the time, seeing it slipping away and neither of the two groups any closer to getting anything accomplished, Steve made a command decision and took the success of one of the groups on his back. Group one, Mark's group.

As they watched in awe, Steve repaired the fence almost single-handedly, with one or two offering to hold things in place as he swung the hammer or hauled the logs.

Completing the task, Steve checked his watch. Fifteen minutes remained. He moved to group two and judged their progress, then with the time he had left, he finished theirs as well.

"Time!" Petula shouted as she moved front and center.

Catching his breath, gulping water from a bottle, Steve

had taken off his t-shirt and used it as a towel to wipe his face and chest from the dripping sweat.

"Who won?" she asked him.

Watching group two grow angry and hearing their, "Oh, but he had to help them first," comments, Steve crushed the empty plastic bottle of water in his fist and said, "It was a tie."

"A tie? Well, then, beer and wine for everyone!" she shouted.

A loud whooping cheer rang out as everyone high-fived and clapped, then hurried to the chow tent for dinner and booze.

Mr. Parsons walked over to where Steve was sitting and recuperating. In anticipation of a brow-beating, Steve winced and peeked up at him. "So, now that you witnessed my crappy leadership skills... Am I fired?"

Mr. Parsons sat next to him on the large boulder. "What you lacked in motivation skills, you gained in teaching by example. You showed them how to do it, and that it could be done. Then, instead of favoring one group over the other, you wanted them to share in the victory together. The result was not a group divided, but a group united."

"I had no idea it would be that hard to get them to do it."

"They're a pampered bunch, Steve. They don't use their hands for a living other than typing on a computer and dialing a phone. Not everyone is in the shape you are."

Steve looked down at those hands of his. They were bloody from blisters that had burst.

"Well done. Get those cuts looked at. Come on...you deserve a beer."

Steve draped his shirt over his right shoulder, then stood up stiffly and walked to the mess tent with Mr. Parsons. As he passed through the entrance, he noticed Mark standing there, as if he were waiting for him. The minute they caught eyes, Mark turned and disappeared inside the busy tent.

"There's a nurse through that door. She'll help you out."

"Thanks, Harold." Steve knocked on the door adorned

with a large red cross, then he opened it. "Hi. I'm wounded." He showed her his hands.

The nurse waved him to sit down, and he did, relishing the cool air-conditioning.

Once he was given some band-aides for his blisters, he put his shirt back on and entered the tent. By the sound of the raucous laughter and mirth, he knew the booze was being applied liberally. Charlie and Kevin spotted him, waving him over. Steve nodded he'd seen them, then filled up a plate with food, and stuck a beer in his fist.

"Nice one, Steve!" Charlie raised his beer up in a toast. "I had no idea you had it in you."

Chewing a buttered roll ravenously, Steve swallowed it down with some ale, then found Mark standing near them, staring at him.

"I felt like such a wimp!" Kevin laughed, "I couldn't even lift that stupid hammer up. I tried, Steve, honest. How the hell did you get so strong? Is it from being a cop? Do they make you work out or something?"

"If you're strong you live." He shrugged. "I suppose that was something that rubbed off on me in the academy." He chewed his hamburger, then found Mark's eyes on him again.

"Christ, Miller," Charlie shook his head. "I wouldn't want to be in a fight with you."

Smiling, flattered, Steve then searched once again for Mark and didn't see him. "Uh, did Richfield already eat?"

Charlie and Kevin looked around the room for him. "I don't know," Charlie said, then resumed consuming his meal. "No need for a beer run."

"No. No need." Steve continued to eat, keeping an eye out for any sign of the Brit.

After the meal, Steve headed for the men's shower facility. A towel and his kit of toiletries in his hand, he entered the locker-type room and set his things down on a

31

bench. Peeling off the band-aides gingerly, he checked his hands out, then sighed and stripped for the shower. He entered a stall and tested the water. As he shampooed his hair he tried to think of how to apologize to Mark. It was beginning to gnaw at him and he needed to get it straightened out.

Rinsed and wrapped in a towel, he set his kit on the sink and decided to shave now instead of back in the tiny toilet at the room. After spreading foam on his face, and seeing several other men coming and going to do the same as he, he caught sight of Mark's reflection in the mirror. The razor suspended in his hand, he watched as Mark set his things down and kicked off his shoes. Spinning around, Steve shouted, "Mark!"

He raised his head and then his expression soured instantly. "Piss off."

"Wait...Mark..." Steve moved a few steps towards him.

Mark stripped off his shorts and shirt angrily and stormed into one of the shower stalls, pulling the plastic curtain shut with a snap.

Sighing tiredly, Steve moved back to the mirror and finished shaving, then wiped off the foam from his face with the towel and slipped his shorts back on. Scuffing back to the room, he found it blissfully empty. He stripped down to his briefs, then lay back on the bedspread, staring at the ceiling. By the time Mark had made it back to the room, he was asleep.

Chapter Five

The next morning they were back in the classroom, in a circle, with the pad and markers at the ready. Yawning through another three hours of useless talking, Steve rubbed his face and wished he were home. In his humble opinion, everyone was worn out from the heat and weariness of the lectures, and no one was gaining a thing.

Too much caffeine in his blood from the never-ending flow of black coffee, Steve craved healthy food, anything other than Wagon Train grub. Standing in line at the mess tent, he curled his nose at the selection of meat, meat, potatoes, bread, meat, and then more meat. Kevin filled his plate with enthusiasm behind him. Steve twisted over his shoulder to watch him. "How can you eat all that?"

"I love it!" He licked his fingers.

"What the hell is on the agenda for later? I can't keep track."

"Hiking in the Cerrillos Hills? Something like that."

"Oh." Steve reluctantly filled his plate, then noticed some chicken with relief and chose that instead of the ubiquitous beef. As he sat down, Mark stood and left the table, seemingly finished with his meal. Steve tried not to feel sick about it. When he woke that morning, Mark was already gone from the room, missing another chance to talk to him.

Petula walked around to the tables and handed out the

next team-building exercise. Steve set the paperwork down without a glance.

Within an hour they were outside the ranch and handed gaudy cowboy hats, bandanas, and leather belts. Holding up his hat in revulsion, Steve said, "No. Is this a joke?"

"It's for the hot sun. Didn't you read the paperwork?" Charlie popped his on his head.

"You look like a dork." Steve laughed, then tried his on.

"Yeah? Well, you look like a cigarette commercial."

"Oh, that's flattering," Steve snorted in annoyance.

They were handed a small package. Once again Steve didn't pay much attention to it and set it down as he fastened his belt around his shorts, stuffed the bandana into his back pocket and felt ridiculous.

"Get into your groups of four from your room assignments!" Petula hollered over the noise.

Immediately Steve searched for Mark. He found him making his way over reluctantly in his tight khaki shorts and white polo shirt, a beige cowboy hat on his head, his long hair streaming out from underneath and the bandana tied around his neck like a scarf.

"Your instructions are in the packet, so open them now and get started."

Looking back at the tiny brown parcel, Steve picked it up and opened it. "A map," he announced.

"I've got a compass," Charlie said.

Kevin held up a pocketknife.

They waited for Mark. Seemingly already frustrated with his companions, he opened his and found a canteen. He unscrewed the lid and sniffed it. "Water," he said.

"Get going!" Petula waved them off. "Find the treasure and meet back here in three hours!"

"Three hours?" Steve groaned. He looked at the map and then the lay of the land to get an idea of where they were on it. As the other groups disbanded, the three men once again looked to Steve for some guidance.

"Which way is north, Charlie?" he asked.

Setting the compass in his palm, Charlie pointed.

"Let's go." Steve stuffed the folded map into his shorts' pocket, adjusted the brim of his hat to shield the sun's glare, then marched off.

Within an hour, Mark was handing around the canteen, and Steve stood with the map, scratching his hot head under the hat. "That way...I think."

"You think?" Mark snapped at him. "An hour of bloody wandering and 'you think' it's that way? Are you having a laugh? Give me the flamin' map!" He snatched it out of Steve's hand.

Crossing his arms over his chest, Steve glared at him, trying to be patient and wait before he strangled someone.

"Right...which way's north, Charles?" Mark asked.

Charlie took out the compass. "That way." He pointed, adjacent to the sun which was moving west.

"Right...it shows a hill here, and a group of Juniper trees there...pinon...what the bloody hell is a pinon?"

"A snake?" Kevin replied. When three weary glares met his gaze, he smiled weakly.

Mark looked back at the map. "If we walk a few meters from that point, there should be some flag or something marking a spot."

In a sarcastic gesture, Steve waved his hand, saying, "Lead on!"

"How far is a meter?" Charlie whispered to Kevin.

Steve could only shake his head sadly.

Fifteen minutes later, Mark was looking bewildered. Steve rolled his eyes at the folly.

"My turn." Kevin took the map. "Let me see...where the hell are we?"

"Give me that!" Steve took it back and exhaled tiredly. "Limey here has completely led us astray—"

"Oh, fuck you, ya bleedin' wanker!" Mark snarled.

"Well?" Steve waved around. "Where the hell are we now, Richfield?"

"Uh oh," Kevin gulped, "please don't tell me we're

lost."

"We're not bloody lost." Mark brooded.

"Yes, thanks to you, we are 'bloody' lost." Steve took off his hat and wiped the sweat off his forehead.

"Thanks to me?" Mark shouted in rage, "I take over for a minute and now it's my fault we're lost? You taking the mick?"

"Taking the what?" Steve shook his head in irritation. "Look, just shut up and let me look at it."

With Mark tapping his toe on the dirt, Charlie licking his dry lips, and Kevin on the verge of panic, Steve hated to admit he could not make heads or tails of the little map, and in his opinion, they had strayed very far off course. "Let's just back track."

"Okay," Charlie replied.

"Which way's south?" Steve asked.

Charlie read the compass and pointed.

"No," Steve said, "It can't be. We were headed that way and we were going north."

"It says that way is south."

The other three looked over Charlie's shoulder at the tiny gauge. Steve said, "Can I see it for a sec?"

Charlie handed it over.

After spinning around in all directions, Steve tossed it to Charlie and sighed, "We're fucked."

"What?" came out in a desperate chorus.

"It's not working right. Couldn't you tell that no matter which way we were moving, the needle never moved?" Steve sat down on a large rock and asked Mark, "Can I have a sip of that water?"

He unfastened it from his belt and handed it off to him.

Steve wet his mouth and took a small sip. "Listen, guys, if we are lost, this water has to last, so no greedy mouthfuls. Just a tiny sip. Got it?"

"We're ganna die!" Kevin shouted, waving his arms around.

"Shut the fuck up." Steve rubbed his face and rough jaw

tiredly. "We're not going to die, you moron."

"I can't last out here!" Kevin wailed. "I'm going back!"

As he darted off in an ambiguous direction, Charlie looked back at Mark and Steve in horror. Steve shrugged and said, "His problem."

"Nice team spirit, Miller!" Charlie raced after Kevin.

When their footfalls faded away, Steve sat calmly and stared at the setting sun. Hearing Mark clear his throat, he turned to look at him.

Mark had removed his hat and was running his fingers through his long hair. "Should I be nervous?"

"Naaa…" Steve reclined back over the rock and covered his face with his hat.

"Then we're not lost?"

Rolling to his side, Steve took off his hat and sighed, "I'm not sure. I'm just not the type to panic easily. Look, Richfield, they have measures in place at these things. Soon someone in a jeep will be by and pick us up."

"You think so?"

"Yeah," he replied, then lay back and closed his eyes, covering them with his hat again.

Feeling disoriented, Steve woke up to hear someone ranting and raving nearby.

"We're not lost, he said! Someone will be by! Just wait and a jeep will pick us up! Well? Where's the bloody jeep?"

Steve rubbed his face and focused on Mark as he paced nervously. Checking his watch first, Steve then noticed the sun ready to dip below the hilly horizon.

As soon as Mark realized he was awake, he shouted, "You bloody idiot! No one is on their way! We're flamin' lost! Do you feel how cold it's getting? Look! Look! I've got goose flesh! Look!" He showed Steve his forearm. "I'm not equipped for this! And what about snakes? Pinon? Is that a snake? What about scorpions? Oh, we had to listen to the bloody LAPD cop! Bloody wanker is more like!"

Sitting up in anger, Steve shouted back at Mark, "Pinon is a type of tree, you dipshit, not a snake. I said don't worry! What the hell is wrong with you? Are you really that soft that you can't take an hour in the desert to cool off? For cryin' out loud, Richfield. How pampered are you?"

"How pampered?" Mark railed, "Very! Very fucking pampered, mate! I come from a very wealthy background! My parents have title, breeding! I can't sit on my arse out here in the cold! And it's your bleedin' fault! You think you're so bloody macho and strong that you can run over everyone around you. Oh, make no mistake, mate, no one has a say when you're in the room."

Steve stood up and puffed out his chest in rage. "What the hell are you talking about?"

"What the hell? What the hell?" Mark mimicked in fury. "What did you do in the team building exercise? Eh? Did you motivate the group? Did you get everyone to cooperate? No! Ya bloody did it all yourself to prove how flamin' manly you were! *Oh, there's Officer Miller showing off his biceps.* You weren't impressing anyone, mate. There were no single birds there to ogle you. Just a few married female executives who put up with your arrogant display."

"Shut the fuck up!" Steve roared. "No one did a fucking thing! You pussies are too soft for holding an axe or a hammer. Which one of you volunteered? Huh? *You* didn't! You were afraid you'd break a nail, for cryin' out loud. Don't act as if you stepped up to the plate and helped out."

"It was a team exercise, you wanker! A bloody team building exercise! What did you do? You played Mr. Flamin' Macho-man. We were all impressed, Officer Miller. Oh, yes…we now worship the ground you walk on!"

"You think I wanted to kill myself out there? In the grueling sun? Look at my fucking hands!" He held them up in front of Mark's face. "You see the damn blisters I've got? You think it was fun?"

"A small price to pay for your ego."

"And I felt guilty!" Steve threw up his hands in a comic

gesture. "I actually wanted to apologize to your sorry ass about what I said earlier. Ya know what? You can fuck yourself!" Steve stormed off.

Immediately he could hear Mark's footsteps behind him. Stopping, he turned around in exasperation.

His arms crossed over his chest to fend off the chill, Mark's eyes were wide in the dimming light. "You're not leaving me alone out here."

Taking a moment to gather his thoughts, Steve climbed up a nearby hill and had a look around. "Jesus, it's fucking dark."

"Can you see anything? A light in the distance, perhaps?"

"No. You would think I could see the damn ranch, but who knows which direction it's in."

"It's got to be that one. I'm as certain as you we were headed this way," he pointed behind him, "...and should be heading that way now. I'm not a bloody fool. I know where the sun sets."

"And it has set." Steve sighed and walked back over to where Mark was standing. "Look, we can't wander around in the dark. Let's just park here and wait till morning."

When Steve sat down on the dirt, Mark shouted, "Here? Sit here? Are you joking? Are you suggesting we sleep in the rough? On the ground? Oh, you are winding me up...you can't be serious."

"Shut up, limey, and sit down." Steve set his hat next to him and rubbed his head.

After a reluctant minute, Mark plopped down beside him. "It's bloody cold."

Steve nodded. "It's amazing how the temperature dips after the sun sets."

"Don't you feel cold?" Mark shivered and rubbed his legs, hugging them to his body.

"Of course I do. I'm just not a wimp."

"Will you stop playing the bloody hero? It's wearing on me nerves!"

Ignoring him, Steve brushed some stones away from the ground behind him and lay back, staring at the sky as stars began to appear.

"I'll end up bit by a bloody snake." Mark looked around him in paranoia.

Steve laughed to himself, but he knew Mark heard it. Finally he said, "Just lie back and enjoy the view. Look at that. How often do you see that kind of sky without the ambient light of the cities ruining it?"

Mark tilted upwards.

As Steve watched, Mark managed to get horizontal as if the ground revolted him. It took some time, but he finally heard Mark sigh in awe at the sight.

Steve smiled, "Amazing, huh?"

"Quite."

"Bet you don't see that in England."

"No. I can't say I have. I never knew there were that many stars up there."

"It's covered in stars. We only usually see the brightest ones."

"Fuck, why is it so cold? I was burning up only a moment ago."

"Where's the canteen?"

"Here." Mark showed him. He shook it and they both heard water inside.

"Use it as a pillow."

"Oh. All right." Mark made sure the cap was secure, then propped it in back of his head.

In the silence, Steve enjoyed the cosmic view. "I used to love stargazing as a boy."

"Did you? Not shooting birds in the woods?"

Turning his head to see his profile in the dim light, Steve asked, "What the hell kind of a monster do you think I am?"

"I don't know you well enough to guess."

"I'm actually a nice guy."

"Oh? Have that on your curricular vitae?"

"My what?"

"Never mind," Mark snorted.

"I'm not stupid either, Mark. I didn't get where I am today because I'm an idiot. Contrary to what you think."

"And where are you today, Miller? Hmm? Lost in the flippin' desert? Well done!"

"You're lost too, limey! It's not all me to blame!"

"It's your country! Not mine! And who had the bloody map?" Mark sat up.

"Who had the 'bloody' broken compass?" Steve sneered.

"Oh, shut up...I've a bleedin' headache. I'm half starved."

"You are so soft, it's sickening."

"Oh, so sorry I offend the brutish police officer. Why don't you just beat me up and get your jollies?"

"I should. At least it would warm me up and shut you up." Steve laughed sarcastically.

"Go on then!" Mark dared, "Hit me! You've been hungry for it since we met. You're so bloody paranoid I'll take that account. And I will...oh, bloody yes, I will."

Steve sat up abruptly and faced him. "You will not! I worked my ass off for that account and I'm not going to see some pansy-ass limey take it from me!"

"You will see me take it! Are you joking? I've just about got it now! Parsons is very smitten by me. I know who'll get it."

"You fucking bastard! Smitten? Just because you're good looking he's supposed to go for you? What the hell's that supposed to mean? He's a married man with grandchildren, you weirdo!"

"What? I don't like what you're implying! You implied the same thing when you said I'd suck his bloody cock! Who do you think you are?"

"I'm the one whose about to kill you, that's who I am!" Steve got to his knees and tensed up.

"Kill me? Oh, go ahead! It's the only way you'll ever get the bloody Foist account! You can't do it on merit! So, go ahead, Miller! Try and kill me!"

41

Steve grabbed his shoulders and shoved him back to the ground. Mark gripped his arms and braced him up off his body. They wrestled around the dusty earth, trapping each other's legs and trying to pin down arms and control fingers and knees. When Steve realized their hips were connected he had a flash of fire wash over him that stunned him.

"Come on, you bleedin' cop! This the best you can do?"

"You're stronger than you look, you stupid limey!"

"Am I?" Mark laughed cruelly. "Or are you not as tough as you look?"

"I don't want to really hurt you, that's all!" Steve ground his jaw and struggled with him, unable to stop rubbing his hard cock against Mark's crotch.

"Oh? Is that your excuse? Kill me, but don't hurt me? You flippin' moppet! You're all talk!"

"Shut up! Just shut the fuck up!" Something in Steve broke. An incredible animal attraction for this man was making his head spin and he would be humiliated if Mark felt how hard he had gotten from the contact. He shoved him back and twisted away.

"Thought so," Mark sneered, brushing off his legs and arms. "Nothing but bravado. You're pathetic."

Wiping at his tears discreetly, Steve felt sick inside. As if everything that had come before this was meaningless and a failure, he began to travel back in time remembering everything that had ever gone wrong in his life.

Wiping off his face in humiliation with the bandana he removed from his pocket, Steve peeked behind him in embarrassment.

Mark was curled up on the dirt, trying to keep warm, with his back facing him. The sensation of the friction of Steve's body humping on his reverberated through his crotch making him rock hard. Images of Steve wielding the axe and hammer, shirtless, raced through his mind. There was no doubt Steve was hot. Very hot indeed. But how could he get excited by his touch? It didn't make sense. Angry at himself for not loathing the contact between them, Mark imagined nestling up to Steve in the cold night, inhaling his scent, and...*no, no, no*! he chided himself. *You and this man are adversaries, not potential lovers! Use your head!*

Mark bit his lip to control his emotions. Hadn't everyone always assumed he was gay? Hadn't he fought those feelings with everything he had? Was this a test? Was some all-knowing force giving him this incredibly masculine man, dangled in front of him like a carrot, to see if he could be swayed?

Oh, yes. He was swayed. He had not passed the test.

Using his hat as a pillow, Steve gave Mark his back as well, and tried to stop the stream of useless frustration from making him emotional again.

He had fallen asleep. A movement behind him woke him. A warm back had made its way to contact him in the cold night, shivering to keep warm. Opening his eyes, he came around a little more and heard the noises of the dark: a distant coyote, toads, night owls. Then he heard Mark's teeth chattering. Sighing tiredly, he rolled over and tried to wrap around him to warm him up. At first Mark stiffened and seemed to want to push him away, but he was too cold to fight it. Like spoons, they enveloped each other fending off the chill. With his warm breath, Steve puffed on the back of Mark's neck through his long hair. Inhaling deeply, Steve caught its fragrant aroma and closed his eyes as it filled his senses. A tiny moan escaped Mark's lips, as if he finally, gratefully, felt the warmth he craved. Steve tightened his arms around him, feeling the size and strength of Mark's body. With his left hand, he rubbed Mark's shoulder and upper arm, warming him.

In his embrace he felt Mark relax slightly from the relief. He rubbed his elbow, his forearm, feeling his cold skin.

Then he caressed his hip, then the long solid thigh that had curled up into a fetal position for warmth. With his palm Steve warmed that leg, running over his shin, his knee, then back up his thigh to the edge of Mark's shorts. Steve shivered, but not from a chill. He closed his eyes and nestled into that soft long hair, inhaling him like a drug. Without a conscious thought, he moved his hand to that belt and opened it. Next was a button, then a zipper. Mark tensed up and gripped Steve's wrist. Steve wrenched out of that grip and found the waistband of Mark's shorts, pulling them down his backside roughly. Mark rolled over violently, grabbing Steve's arms to stop him. Then, in the dimmest of moonlight, their eyes met. As Steve's heart pounded like a kettle drum in his chest, he waited what felt like hours, but must only have been seconds. When Mark's mouth made contact with his, he thought his brain would explode from the thrill. Steve stripped Mark, pushing his shorts down his pelvis and began undoing his own zipper. With that exotic British tongue in his mouth he released his cock and whimpered in longing.

When Mark pulled back to catch his breath, Steve shoved him over, onto his face, then thrust his hips against that tight muscular backside, yearning to penetrate it. Feeling Mark tighten his legs to solid muscle to trap his cock, Steve pumped feverishly into that tight gap, his hips hammering between those smooth thighs and under his balls. As he came he bared his teeth and clamped his eyes shut. Before he had a chance to inhale a gasping breath, Mark had him lying flat, stuffing his own cock between Steve's large thighs. Mark braced himself with his arms, arching his back and pumping his hips as Steve looked up at that angular jaw and that long hair, a halo around an angel's face. A deep guttural "Ah!" sound emerged from that perfect mouth. Hot sticky cum ran down Steve's inner thighs. With both his strong arms he wrapped around Mark, bringing him closer to lie against his chest, then hunted down that mouth again. Sucking on it, going wild for it,

44

they rolled around the solid ground, rubbing their naked hips against each other igniting fire after fire. Steve felt tears running down his dirt-stained cheeks, dug his fingers into that thick head of hair and felt as if he couldn't get enough of that taste, that scent, that naked body rubbing against his.

"Oh, Christ..." Steve cried between kisses, "Oh, Christ, oh, Christ..."

"You're divine...absolutely spectacular..." Mark moaned, wrapping around him, licking his face, his neck.

Panting, unable to catch his breath, Steve lay still with Mark on top of him, their legs intertwined, their cocks nestled together. Opening his eyes, Steve could just make out Orion's belt in the vast sky above them. Then he heard Mark sigh, "I'm bloody boiling now."

Slowly his smile worked into a chuckle, then a full belly laugh. "Oh, Christ, Richfield, you are high maintenance."

Mimicking his accent, Mark replied, "Oh, Christ, Miller, you are right." Mark wiggled on Steve as they rested, then he whispered, "You are one horny cop."

"I'm not a cop anymore, Mark," Steve almost whined in exhaustion.

Leaning up to see his face, Mark said, "But it'd be sexier if you were."

"Are you gay?"

"No. Are you?"

"No." Steve laughed.

"I reckon we are now." Mark poked his hard cock against Steve, eager for more.

"I suppose." Feeling the poking, Steve smiled, "And you think I'm horny?"

"You are." Mark caressed his face.

"You're the one sticking his cock into me."

"Oi? No, horny...sexy."

"Oh, here horny means hot to trot."

"That's randy."

"Who's randy?"

"You are."

"What?" Steve tilted his head. "I'm not called Randy."

"Oh, shut your gob and kiss me. I'm cooling off again."

"High maintenance!" Steve laughed, then wrapped around him again.

"Are we mad?" Mark asked after their kiss.

"Yes." Steve nodded emphatically.

"Will we hate ourselves in the light of day?"

"Oh, yes." Steve nodded again, with more conviction.

"Forget it. Shag me again."

"Come here, limey." Steve grabbed his face and kissed him.

Chapter Six

Steve opened his eyes. The brightness felt blinding. Getting his mind to ignite with reason, he blinked a few times and then raised his head off the ground to see long brown hair cascading over his chest. "Oh, fuck," he breathed as the nighttime activities began to come back to him. "Mark…Mark, wake up."

Groggy with sleep, Mark lifted his head off Steve's chest and tried to open his eyes. "Where the bleedin' hell am I?"

Steve checked his watch, then sat up. "You have that canteen?"

"Oi? Oh, yes." Mark found it and handed it to him.

Steve took a drink, then dabbed a drop on his bandana and wiped his face with it.

Groaning as if he were stiff, Mark slowly stood up and stretched his back. "Look, Steve…about last night…"

"Oh, don't worry. I'm not saying a word! And you better not either… Wait… What's that?" Steve perked up.

"What's what?" Mark moaned and tried to straighten out his shirt, tucking it into his shorts.

Jumping to his feet, Steve ran up that hill again and began shouting. "A jeep! Mark, a jeep!" Hopping up and down, they managed to flag their rescuers and then stood a moment to look at each other.

"You're a filthy mess," Mark said, shaking his head at him.

Steve looked down at himself. "Same as you, buddy."

"No! I look that bad?" Mark began brushing off his clothing. Dust billowed off them in tiny clouds.

"Christ…I hope they don't think we did anything." Steve used the bandana to keep wiping at his skin.

Before Mark could reply, Mr. Parsons jumped out of the passenger seat of the jeep, appearing very relieved. "I'm so glad you're both in one piece!"

"Yes…" Steve tried to smile, picking his hat up off the ground. "The compass was bad. Did you find Kevin and Charlie?"

"Oh, yes. They made it back last night. We did a search for you then, but gave up. It was really too dark to continue."

With his mouth gaping open, Mark gasped, "Kevin and Charles made it back?"

"Yes!" Mr. Parsons gestured for them to get into the jeep. "Come boys, back to the ranch so you can clean up."

Steve caught Mark's fury aimed at him. "What?" Steve asked as he sat down in the back seat.

With his teeth showing under his curled lip, Mark didn't answer.

The driver sped over the hilly landscape as Mr. Parsons chatted relentlessly about the new day's events and the wrapping up of the retreat. Mark had his arms crossed tightly over his chest in rage, as Steve tried to tune everything out and pretend he was home.

When they arrived back at the ranch they had a welcoming party of almost a dozen co-workers. Charlie and Kevin raced over to them and wasted no time in teasing them.

"You should have followed us!" Kevin shouted, "We got back in time for dinner! Why didn't you come with us?"

Charlie elbowed Steve in the ribs and whispered, "A little *Brokeback Mountain* thing going on?"

"Shut up," Steve snarled.

As Mark stormed off to the showers he was throwing up

his hands in frustration and muttering, "I had to stick with the cop! I had to sleep on the bloody ground!"

Finally under a spray of hot water and lathered in soap, Steve closed his eyes and kept getting waves of sensuous pleasure from remembering last night. Every time Mark felt the cold, he rolled on top of him and began grinding his hips against his. He lost track of how many times he had come. His cheeks and lips felt tender from Mark's five o'clock shadow.

Leaning both hands on the cement wall, the water pummeling his face and hair, Steve closed his eyes and replayed the sex again and again until he was lightheaded from it. Though he never penetrated him, he craved it and wondered if he would ever achieve that goal. Moving his right hand lower, he held himself and imagined he was back on that hard dirty ground shoving his cock between those masculine thighs, sucking that mouth, teased by that tongue. It was the most intense sexual experience he had ever had. And he wanted more.

Mark had finished getting dressed, combing his wet hair out in the bathroom mirror in their room. Images kept surging over him of the contact he and Steve had in the night. And it was making him so excited he could barely function. Guilt had crept in as well. Thinking of the phone call he had made earlier to someone back home was giving him a headache. The moaning and complaining he had been enduring lately was getting on his nerves. *Couldn't he get anything done? Couldn't he be more like this or more like that?* It was enough to make him shout out in anger. Instantly he had regretted calling and checking in. And the resentment of that insatiable controlling demand was angering him.

They were fed, clean, and back in a classroom by ten a.m. Though Steve felt compelled to talk to Mark, get his comments on the night's events, Mark seemed unapproachable, preoccupied, and out of reach.

Mr. Parsons stood in front of the class this time and smiled grandly at what he considered a very good group of employees. "I can't tell you all how proud I am of you. You all worked together and got along brilliantly. I knew this retreat would be a tonic for a wonderful crew like you, and I'm glad I made the investment." He paused and looked around the room, then met Steve's eyes. "However, there is one thing we have yet to reveal…"

Steve's stomach went cold and hard.

"Though it seemed as if a bit of bad luck had found your group," Mr. Parsons grinned slyly at Steve, then at Mark. "It was a trick, and it seems unfair to not reveal it to you."

Complete disorientation filled Steve. Even Mark looked back at him curiously, as if to ask what was going on.

Seeing their confusion easily, Mr. Parsons nodded to Charlie to explain. Enthusiastically Charlie stood up and held out the compass. "We knew it was broken, Miller."

Steve still wasn't getting it, and it appeared to him, neither was Mark.

As if Kevin felt he couldn't keep quiet, he shouted, "It was planned, Steve, Mark! It was all planned to see if you guys could get along!"

Feeling his skin crawl, Steve had nightmarish images of hidden cameras and incriminating videos. He heard Mark gasp, "Wha-at?" in shock.

Mr. Parsons continued, "And you came through well. You used team work to get through the night and managed to stay together and work in partnership instead of fighting and going your separate ways. I'm very proud of you both. Steve… Stand up and tell the group how you and Mark managed to get over your adversarial relationship to come through with flying colors."

Meeting Mark's petrified *if you say anything I'll kill you* stare, Steve had a very difficult time actually standing up. "Uh…"

"Don't be shy, Steve," Mr. Parsons prodded.

His hands finding the insides of his shorts pockets, Steve coughed, cleared his throat and tried to look at anyone but a pale Mark Richfield. "We…uh…we just dealt with it. There isn't much more to say. We decided to stay put."

"Go on," Mr. Parsons said, waving.

"Uh…you know…uh…we figured it was better not to separate or get any more lost. I knew eventually someone would find us. Well, and in the end we weren't that far from the ranch."

Mr. Parsons aimed his stare at Mark. "Mark, tell us more. Did you allow Steve to take the lead?"

Thinking it couldn't be possible, Steve watched Mark lose even more color from his cheeks. "Pardon?" Mark replied, as if he didn't understand the question.

"The lead," Mr. Parsons repeated. "Did you defer to his judgment?"

"Oh…that…uh…at times. Well, he was a police officer, and this is his country. I just thought it stood to reason."

"Well done!" Mr. Parsons shouted. "It just goes to show you, anything is possible."

Immediately Steve found Mark's light eyes. When they connected, there was a bolt of electricity between them, but Steve had no idea how to read his expression.

The next hour was full of accolades and the promise of good working policy and rewards for achieved goals. Steve had already lost interest and was back in the desert on Mark's naked buttocks.

By late afternoon they were finally cut free. The bus was to depart the next morning at six a.m. More alcohol was provided in the food tent and talk of work morphed into talk of frivolity and the rest of the world.

Sated on too many beers, Steve found his weary way back to the room to take a break from all the conversations.

When he opened the door he found Mark packing his bag, folding things neatly and placing them in the case with care. At the sound of the door, he raised his chin to have a look.

"Hi."

"Hi," Mark mumbled, then went back to his packing.

"Uh…I didn't see you in there…did you eat?"

"I had a bit. I wasn't in the mood for the natter."

"Natter?"

"Talk…conversations."

"Oh." Steve sat down on Mark's bed and watched as he packed his things.

Once he had filled it with all his belongings, Mark picked the suitcase up off the bed and set it next to a dresser on the floor. "Did you want something?"

Moving his gaze from the bedspread pattern to those forlorn green irises, Steve wanted to say *you* but couldn't even begin to mouth the word. "Just keeping you company."

Gracefully sitting down near him, Mark folded his hands on his lap and a deep sigh escaped him. Then he whispered, "Steve…"

Holding up his hand, Steve cut him off, "Don't."

"But…I…"

"Mark…stop. Look, it was just a crazy night. It was the cold or something. I know." Forcing himself to look at his face, Steve inhaled and raised his lowered eyelids. Mark's mouth had formed a grim line, his eyes appeared luminous and wet. Instantly Steve's skin covered with chills as he visualized pushing him back on the mattress and rubbing every part of his body against him. A painful sound emerged from his chest before he could prevent it. He tore his eyes away and stood off that bed.

Before either one could say another word, the door opened behind them and a very drunk Charlie and Kevin entered, each holding a bottle of wine. Charlie stopped short and slurred, "Oooh! You two lovebirds want to be alone?"

"Shut up!" Steve snapped in fury as Mark just turned his

face away in shame.

"*Brokeback Mountain*!" Charlie taunted, "I can see it! Two virile hunks out in the hills humping—"

Steve had him by the throat so quickly the wine bottle dropped from Charlie's hand and rolled away. Kevin just blinked his eyes in astonishment at Steve's anger, while Mark never turned around to look.

With his veins bulging in his arms and neck, Steve growled with pure venom, "If I hear that once more from you, Richards, I'll beat you so hard you'll wish I killed you."

Charlie choked for breath and tried to pry Steve's powerful hands off his neck. "All right! Man, it's just for a laugh!"

"Let him go, Steve. He didn't mean anything by it." Kevin touched Steve's back lightly.

As if making a command decision, Steve released Charlie, then marched to the bed and threw his belongings into his suitcase. Right before he stormed out he glanced at Mark. Mark's head was lowered and he was sitting very still. Throwing open the door, Steve never looked back. He slammed his case into the trunk of his car and without a thought to the time or his energy level, he headed back to LA.

Mark sat completely still. With the other two men talking quietly behind him about Steve's departure, Mark wanted to follow Steve out, get away from the suspicious stares, and pretend to the outside world that things didn't go the way they had in that desert.

But he also had the urge to rush after Steve to comfort him, to tell him what he was really going to say was that he was crazy about him. The last thing he wanted to do was tell Steve that what had happened between them didn't matter. It did. It was a monumental moment in Mark's life. He finally understood all the repressed feelings he had been dealing with eternally. It was as if Steve had unlocked the door for him. If nothing else, he wanted to run after him and thank him for it.

Shaking, feeling ill and overtired, Steve came through his front door in the early hours of dawn. He tossed down his keys and suitcase, then made it to his bedroom, stripped and dropped down under the covers. When he was finally still and under the sheets, he burst into sobs and unleashed the dam he had held back for 800 miles. And all he could think about was Mark, and how much he yearned for him.

Chapter Seven

He did nothing all weekend. Sitting in his sunroom, staring out at the view, his coffee going cold, the clock ticking loudly, he had things to do, errands to tend, phone calls to make. He neglected his exercise, his family; he sat. And sat. Thinking and trying not to think. When the phone rang he leapt up and raced to it, then with disappointment in his voice he said, "Oh, it's you."

"Who did you think it was?" Laura asked.

"No one."

"How was the retreat?"

"Long and useless."

"You sound like crap again. Jesus, Steve, what the heck's going on lately? You used to sound so full of energy. You were thrilled to get out of LAPD, you loved that job...uh oh...are you missing Sonja? Is that it?"

"No. I'm not missing Sonja. Will you stop asking me that? You're like a broken record."

"All right, don't bite my head off. You hear from Mom or Dad?"

"No. They don't call here very often. Why?"

"No reason. If you were married and had a kid you wouldn't be able to get rid of them...so, uh, are you dating anyone?"

"No. Look, Laura, I'm really beat...can I call you back another time?"

"Oh, sure...you don't want to come by for dinner? I'm making lasagna."

"No. I'll take a rain-check. Some other time."

"Okay, little brother...just take care of yourself."

"Okay. See ya." He hung up and took a deep breath of air into his lungs. Slowly he straightened his back and returned to the chair he had occupied. Sitting down, he stared out at the view and wiped at a tear from the corner of his eye. "...ohhh, baby..." he breathed painfully, "I know I'm insane, but I want you...oh Christ, I want you..."

Hours later, reclining on his leather sofa, the television on but not in his field of vision, Steve had finished a six-pack of beer and wallowed in self-pity. A pad on his lap, the words "Pro & Con" at the top, a list of reasons, ideas and wishes running down the length. He kept encouraging himself to just confront the man and be honest. "Mark...can we just try a relationship...no-no-no...you sound pathetic! How about, Mark, let's have sex. No strings attached...AUGH!" he screamed and spun the pad off his lap, then snapped the pencil in two and threw it as well.

Sprawled out on his back in the dim room, the ceiling fan spinning causing bursts of refreshing air to hit his naked chest, Steve closed his eyes and parted his knees, then ran his hand over his cotton shorts. Ever since the sex with Mark he was constantly hard thinking about him. Nothing had excited him like this before, nothing. He peeled open his shorts and spread them wide on his pelvis, then reached inside them to wrap his fingers around his cock. His hips rocking into that invisible lover, he masturbated until his head whirled with the orgasm, then hissed Mark's name over and over as cum spattered his chest. Instantly he was seized with grief and covered his face to sob, "God, I'm going nuts...I'm going nuts..."

Chapter Eight

Monday morning Steve went through the motions of his usual routine but the mirror betrayed his true feelings. He appeared pale and unhappy. Even his smile looked misplaced. Parking in his space, looking back at the Mercedes, he paused, wondering if that sexy TVR would pull up at any moment. When too much time elapsed and his expectations were dashed, he scuffed his leather soles to the elevator and tried to feel motivated. After all, they had just had such an inspirational retreat.

As he entered his office it appeared business as usual. Things were functioning as they should be, phones rang, people clicked away at their computers, coffee cups were full and emptying fast.

"Hello, Mr. Miller."

"Hiya, Mary." He set his briefcase down and hung his suit jacket on the back of the door.

"Here's a cup of coffee for you…did you enjoy the retreat? Everyone's buzzing about it."

"Thanks. Just set it on the desk. Yes. It was very interesting."

"You look tired. You okay?"

"Hmm? Yes. Fine. Anything pressing, Mary? Any calls I need to make right away?"

She handed him some messages from the few days he had missed. He thanked her and watched as she left and closed his door. When he was left alone, he rubbed his face to wake up, then sipped the coffee as he booted up the computer on his desk.

By mid-morning he was in the lounge refilling his cup.

"Hey, Steve."

He spun around and replied, "Hey, Kevin. You recover from that crazy retreat?"

"Yeah…you know, I actually thought it was okay in the end. It wasn't really as bad as I thought it would be."

Steve waited until he poured his own cup of coffee. "Was it really a set up? Getting me and Mark lost?"

Laughing, Kevin put his hand up as if swearing an oath. "Honest to god! We were sworn to secrecy."

"But, what would you have done if we had followed you?"

"We had to lose you. We were going to dart off or something."

"But how did you know how to get back?"

"I kept cutting up bits of this neon colored paper they gave me. You know, with that utility knife. I just followed the trail I had left, picking up the pieces as we went so you didn't find it."

"You suck," Steve said, but laughed.

"Sorry, Parsons' orders." He sipped the hot coffee. "I think he really thought you guys would have a terrible fight. In some ways, you proved him wrong. I swear, Steve, I was afraid if you guys didn't get along he would fire one of you."

"Really? You think he took it that seriously?"

"Yes. I do. He was really stern about making sure we didn't let on. But, you guys did great, so I wouldn't worry…uh, did you guys fight at all? I mean, you seemed to really hate each other."

Smiling to himself, Steve said over his mug of coffee, "I can't tell. I'll get the axe."

"Ha, I knew it. I had a bet with Charlie you'd beat the crap out of each other by nightfall."

"We almost did."

"Shit. You'd kill him." Kevin laughed.

"No. Not really. The guy is very strong."

"Really? I had you pegged as the winner of that battle. Oh well, live and learn. It all worked out in the end."

"Did it? We still don't know who's getting the Foist account."

"Yeah, but at least now you won't hate each other over it." Kevin nodded as he left the lounge.

Leaning back on the counter, Steve drank his coffee and wondered if that was true.

He was just packing up his things and shutting down the computer when he noticed Mark walking past his office. "Mark!" he shouted, racing to catch him.

Mark stopped and turned around.

"Uh, ya got a minute?"

"What for?"

"Uh...just to talk."

Looking around them first, Mark then asked in a lowered voice, "What is there to talk about?"

"What...? Oh, come on!" Steve laughed nervously.

After another paranoid glance around, Mark whispered, "Really, Steve, think of the impropriety."

"Why? You're a co-worker...why can't we have a chat?"

"Oh? You want to know how many references to *Brokeback Mountain* I have heard so far today?"

That enraged Steve. "Who said it?"

"Why? So you can strangle them like you did Charles? Come now, Steve. Act like an adult about it."

"Why should I? They aren't."

"Good-bye, Steve."

"Mark..." Steve grabbed his arm.

Again, Mark took a very paranoid look around the halls. "For fuck's sake! What are you doing?"

"Please...one minute...in my office." Steve didn't release his grip.

"Bloody hell," Mark mumbled under his breath. "Keep the bleedin' door open," he warned. "I've had enough of the gossip, honest, I'm about to go off me head."

"Fine...keep the damn door open. Get in here." Steve dragged him in and peeked out of the door once he did. Now that he finally had him alone to talk to him, Steve's list of comments dried up. It was as if he were just about to go on stage and could not for the life of him remember one line. *Who am I again? What am I supposed to say?*

Mark folded his arms over his chest, appeared very impatient, tapped the toe of his pointy Italian leather shoe and waited. When nothing was produced from Steve's mouth but inhaled sighs and one syllable grunts, he threw up his hands comically. "What?"

"Wait..." Steve felt as if he was hyperventilating. All he wanted to say was how much he needed him, wanted him, had to have him.

"Look, Steve...everyone got their laugh, right? Water under the bridge...let's forget the whole thing." He turned to the door.

Unable to get anything out of his mouth, Steve resorted once again to his hands. When he gripped Mark, this time Mark grew angry. "Look, mate, I don't know what you're playing at!"

Someone peered into the office curiously at the shout.

Both men panicked. Mark left the room quickly. Steve was left to make the excuses. "Uh, sorry, he was just in a rush...had to get home."

In the emptiness of that office, he clenched his fists in anguish and cursed silently. Why couldn't he just say what he had to say and screw the consequences? But that was easier said than done.

The lights were beginning to switch off as the office

emptied. Loitering near his office, Steve waited for his opportunity, then moved to Mr. Parsons' secretary's desk. Opening Ray's Rolodex, he thumbed through the cards quickly and found what he was searching for. Glancing around the silent office first, he then copied the information he needed on a post-it note and stuffed it into his pocket. Flipping closed the Rolodex, he took a last look at the desk to ensure it appeared unmolested, then left.

When he was seated in his car he pulled the paper out of his pocket and read the address and phone number. "My old district," he whispered to himself ironically. Starting up the engine, he placed the gear into reverse, backed out of the space, and then headed directly for Sherman Oaks.

Parking his car along the wide roadway in a neighborhood known for its multi-million dollar homes, Steve checked the house number again and then shut the ignition to stare at it. A wall surrounded the property and a wrought iron gate stood guard over the driveway. The home was set back from the street and obscured by large trees. Feeling more like the LAPD cop than the corporate executive at the moment, he climbed out and walked across the street to have a look. A maroon Jaguar was parked in the curved driveway. He examined the intercom and buzzer wondering what kind of reception he would get if he pushed that button boldly. "Fuck it," he mumbled, and stuck his finger on the buzzer. A man's voice asked who it was. "Uh...I'm here to see Mark Richfield. It's Steve from work."

"Who?"

"Steve Miller...I work with him." A clicking sound startled him and then the gate automatically opened, swinging backwards. Taking off his tie as he walked, he opened the buttons of his shirt collar and stuffed the tie into his trouser pocket. When he made his way up to the front door, an attractive blond male was standing there waiting. Steve didn't know what to make of it and felt more awkward with every passing second.

"Hi, uh…is Mark here?"

"No. Not at the moment. You want to come in?"

"Sure. Thanks." Steve stepped into the foyer and admired the high ceilings and minimalist décor. "I'm Steve Miller…I work with Mark over at Parsons & Company"

"Right. I assumed that when you said you worked with him. I'm Jack Larsen."

Steve shook his hand and still couldn't comprehend the connection between this man and Mark. "Uh…is he due back soon?"

"I don't know. He said he had something to do before he came home. Was he expecting you?"

"No. No, he wasn't."

"Come in. You want a drink?"

"All right."

"Name it."

"Beer?"

Jack smiled. "Have a seat. I'll get you one."

After he left Steve wandered around the sunken living room and walked to the sliding doors that revealed an expansive view. Jack returned, holding an iced mug in his hand. Steve thanked him and sat down when Jack gestured for him to. Unable to prevent it, Steve asked, "You guys live together?"

"Yes." Jack sipped his beer, then set it down next to him on a side table.

"Huh…" Suddenly Steve assumed Mark was indeed gay. He wondered why he said he wasn't. "What do you do for a living?"

"Corporate law. I used to be a criminal attorney but I couldn't stand it."

"No. I can understand that. I dated a defense attorney. She finally had enough of that as well."

"Oh? What's her name? Maybe I know her."

"Sonja…Sonja Knight."

"Sonja?"

"Yes." Steve swallowed more beer and tried not to show

his pain over their break up.

"Gorgeous African American lady…" Jack smiled slyly. "Oh, yes. I know her."

"Really? Small world." Steve averted his eyes from those intelligent blue ones and looked around the room. "So, when do you think he'll be home?"

"I can ring his cell phone." Jack stood up and made for a telephone on the desk.

"No!" Steve shouted, then lowered his voice, "No…that's okay. I'll just finish my beer and go. I don't want to bother him."

Puzzled, Jack asked, "Why would it bother him?"

"I don't know…work shit…you know. You have enough all day and you don't want to deal with it at home." Steve chugged the beer down quickly and wiped his lip.

"You should let me call him. He's going out of town tomorrow."

Paying close attention, Steve asked, "Is he?"

"Yes. He's headed to London."

"For how long?"

"Two weeks. I'm surprised if you work with him, you don't know."

"It's not something I would necessarily be privy to, Jack. We don't work that closely together."

"Oh?"

It was as if suspicion had hit this muscular blond suddenly. Was he a jealous lover? Steve could only guess. "I should be going."

"You sure? I know Mark would be upset he missed you." Jack followed him to the front door.

"Oh, I doubt that," Steve mumbled.

"Sorry?" Jack asked.

"Nothing. Thanks for the beer, Jack." Steve reached out to shake his hand.

"No problem. Stop by anytime."

"Thanks." Steve waved to him as he walked back out to the street, his head spinning from all the information, or lack of it. He sat in his car to think. "Well, he's gay and has a lover. That explains a lot." He turned the key in the ignition and drove home with a very heavy heart.

When he came through his door he kicked off his shoes and changed into a pair of gym shorts. Another beer in his fist, he sat down at the kitchen counter and did something he didn't think he would ever do again. He dialed Sonja's number.

"Steve?"

"Yeah. How did you know it was me?"

"It came up on the display on my phone."

"Oh."

"I'm surprised to hear from you."

"Yes…well, I thought you wanted me to leave you alone, you know."

"No. I said we can still be friends—"

"Look, never mind all that. I have a question for you."

"Oh? Doing some detective work?" she asked sarcastically.

"Sort of. You know an attorney named Jack Larsen?"

"Yes. Why?"

"Is he gay?"

After a pause, Sonja asked, "Why? Why do you want to know that?"

"Just answer my question, Sonja. Is he?"

An exhaled breath escaped her, then she whispered, "Yes. He's gay. He's out and open about it. Why? You have to tell me why."

"Shit. I knew it."

"Steve, you're beginning to remind me of your bigoted father. What's going on?"

"Nothing. Thanks for the info, babe."

"Wait, Steve— don't just hang up."

"What do we have to say to each other, Sonja?"

"I don't know. How's the new job? Are you dating anyone?"

"Job's fine, no, I'm not dating anyone. Look, I do have

to go. I didn't want to bother you."

"It's no bother, Steve. Call me anytime."

"Right. Thanks." He hung up and felt sick, missing her. Finishing his beer, he dropped down on the sofa and imagined bursting into tears again. "Why is my life so fucked up?" he moaned.

Chapter Nine

Tuesday morning he parked next to a strange car. Finding Bret at the elevators waiting for it to hit the garage level, Steve greeted him.

"Hey," Bret replied, then as if answering a question he assumed he would be asked, he said, "I'm parking in Richfield's spot. He's going to be in London for two weeks."

"Ah." Steve nodded, smiled briefly, then wondered how everyone in the world knew he was leaving town but him.

"So, uh, you have any trips planned?"

"Me? No. I have a few appointments locally," Steve answered calmly, though he wanted to shout out, "*Trips planned? You think I have an in with the fricken' BBC?*"

In silence they boarded the elevator and rode it to the top floor.

As he walked to his office, something he had done for years, he sensed a vacuum in the building. A void. Mark's presence had vanished, and Steve tried to prepare himself for making it vanish from his mind as well.

But he couldn't. He found himself moving past Mark's office, sniffing the air inside to get a trace of his cologne, getting lost in a daydream as he sat at his desk, and losing focus whenever anyone addressed him and began a conversation.

Two weeks moved at a snail's pace and Steve never thought he would last going to that office daily without Mark there. He wondered if Jack felt the same way in that big house on his own and even entertained the idea of dropping by. But he just couldn't bring himself to. Lord knew what Mark thought when that big blond informed him that his co-worker and office nemesis stopped by for an unexpected visit. Most likely he was infuriated and had to lie to his better half.

The day that Mark was due back, Steve spent extra time shaving and choosing his clothing. A brand new designer suit on his back, shining leather shoes, a gold wristwatch, and a dab of cologne on his neck, it was as if he were meeting Sonja for dinner at one of her ritzy clubs. "Christ, and I thought my dad's reaction to Sonja was bad enough. If he knew I was mooning over some English stud, he'd literally kill me this time." Checking the time, he grabbed his briefcase and keys and locked up the house. On his way into work he listened to the traffic report and grew nervous, as if he were going on a first date or a job interview.

Over the last two weeks he had debated constantly with himself over his feelings, and not only had they not lessened they had grown completely out of control with time. Knowing Mark was indeed gay seemed to open the door to him in some ways. *Okay, Miller, what do you do now knowing he has a boyfriend?* After meeting Jack he felt guilty for it. But would Mark have cheated on Jack if their relationship was a good one? He knew while he was with Sonja, no one could have turned his head. So, if this thing with Jack was love, then Mark would never have done what he did, right?

It was all very confusing to him, and he needed Mark to clear up all the questions he kept asking himself over and over. That's the problem, he needed Mark.

"Man, is that an understatement," he mumbled under his breath.

When he pulled into the parking garage and that shiny TVR was there, he almost creamed his pants. "Yes! Yes!" he chanted. "Oh, baby…I am so glad you're back!"

A huge grin plastered on his face, Steve rode the elevator greeting everyone politely and trying not to pant like a hound dog at the idea of seeing that man once more. Strutting down the corridor smiling and waving at his office co-workers, he was heading directly for Mark's office when Mr. Parsons diverted him.

"Steve…come here a moment."

Nodding obediently, he entered Mr. Parsons' office and stood waiting.

"Sit down…I know I just caught you coming in. Set your briefcase down and have a seat."

Slightly guarded from the urgency of the tone, Steve set the leather valise down and opened the button of his new suit jacket, then sat.

"I've made a decision on the Foist account. I wanted you to be the first to know."

"Oh." He nodded, but kept his expression a blank and waited for the disappointment.

"I've decided you are the man for the job."

"Well, I can understand your…what?" Steve leaned forward in his chair. "I'm sorry, did you say I got the job?"

"Yes. Congratulations." Mr. Parsons reached out his hand over his desk.

Steve took it and shook it, still absorbing the news.

After a pause, Mr. Parsons said, "I thought you'd be more reactive. You know."

Making eye contact with him, Steve laughed softly and then said, "I guess it wasn't what I expected, Harold. I thought surely Mark would get it. You know, after the BBC—"

"No, my boy, you are my choice. I'll have Roland sit down with you and hand over all the files."

"Yes, sir…uh, does Mark know yet?"

"No. Like I said, I wanted to tell you first… Steve, are you all right with my selection?"

"Yes! Yes, I'm thrilled. I'm sorry I seem preoccupied. I just know Mark was counting on it as well. Uh, you mind if I'm the one to break it to him?"

"Will you do it civilly? No rubbing his nose in it?" Mr. Parsons pointed his finger at him, as if warning him.

"I will be very tactful. Yes." Steve rose up and reached out his hand again. "I won't disappoint you, Harold."

"I know I can count on you, my boy."

Lifting his briefcase up, Steve left, stopped by his office to drop it off, then headed directly to Mark's office.

Standing at the partially opened door, Steve was about to rap on it with two knuckles when he noticed Mark on the phone. Mark held up one finger, indicating to wait, then waved Steve to come in and sit while he finished up.

Sitting down on the leather chair in front of his desk, Steve smiled adoringly at him. As Mark spoke and clicked the computer keyboard, Steve relished in the opportunity to stare, admire, ogle, and lick his chops at that gorgeous creature who somehow had completely captured his heart.

"Right," Mark nodded as he said, "Yes, brilliant. I know you'll be very satisfied with the results…yes, I assure you it's been taken care of…"

When Mark's eyes darted to Steve's, Steve smiled warmly and winked. Seeing it fluster Mark slightly, Steve grinned even broader in amusement.

"Right…cheers, mate…cheers…" Mark hung up the phone and then stared back at Steve's unnerving smile. "You all right?"

"Yes."

"What do you want?"

Looking back at the slightly open door first, Steve then leaned across the desk and whispered, "You…I want you, Richfield."

"You want me to do what?"

69

"No…I want you!" Steve repeated, slightly exasperated it wasn't obvious.

"Why did you stop by my place two weeks ago? What did you want coming there to my home?"

Perceiving the comments as cold and unreceptive, Steve sat back and said, "Why did you tell me you weren't gay."

His eyes widening in shock, Mark stood immediately and closed his office door after peering out first. When he moved back to his desk he said, "I am not gay."

Steve laughed at the joke.

"Why are you saying this? I told you…"

"Marrrk…" Steve shook his head sadly. "Jack Larsen is your gay housemate."

"How do you know Jack is gay?"

"My ex-girlfriend knew him. She was a defense attorney too."

"Then you surmised just because I live with a gay man, that I am gay as well?"

Throwing up his hands in amazement, Steve quietly shouted, "No! Because we fucked each other like rabbits in the fricken desert, you dipshit!"

Mark leaned back against his desk and rubbed his face wearily.

Standing up next to him, sniffing his cologne, Steve purred, "I can't stop thinking about it."

"Neither can I."

"Oh?" Steve looked back at the closed door and then touched his long hair, running his fingers through the locks that brushed Mark's suit jacket.

"Why is my life so complicated?" Mark moaned, then dropped his hands and watched as Steve caressed his hair gently.

"It's not that complicated, gorgeous…let's just do it all again." His pulse rate rising, his cock rock hard, Steve was about to screw him on his desk.

"You're touching me." Mark shrank back.

"I know. Is it making you as hot as it's making me?"

"We're at work. Steve, we're in my office, the door is not locked, I have been tormented to death about *Brokeback Mountain*, and my life has become a mess."

Steve backed up, giving him space, then seeing the serious expression on Mark's face, he sat back down and waited for an explanation.

Taking a moment, as if to gather his thoughts, Mark reached out for Steve's hand and then clasped it warmly. "Oh, love…"

Steve brought Mark's hand to his lips to kiss, then stroked it as he paid careful attention to him.

"I…I have a fiancé, love."

"You what?" Steve choked in shock.

"Aye…a woman. It's the last thing you expected, right? Believe me, everyone thinks Jack and I are lovers. No, love. He is gay, yes, but we are not lovers."

Steve never thought he could feel so crushed. "No…no, Mark, you have to be kidding. After that hot passionate sex we had? Are you sure?"

"No. I'm not sure about anything at the moment. I'm a mess. A complete bloody mess. And she's turned on me, love. She's become this demanding creature. It's been going bad for months now, getting worse all the time. I just don't know what the right thing to do is…"

Instantly, Steve rose up and embraced him. As their bodies connected it was as if they suddenly remembered what it felt like, what that touch brought with it.

Steve gripped Mark's smooth jaw and kissed him, sucking at his mouth with so much passion he thought he would devour him. And though at first Mark hesitated, he too succumbed to the fire. Groaning in agony at having him in his arms again, tasting his mouth, inhaling his cologne, Steve couldn't care less if the entire office walked in. He wouldn't care at all.

Groping him, finding that huge cock rock hard under his silk trousers, Steve was going mad for it. Through his clouded brain he heard Mark trying to calm them down.

71

"Love…baby…all right…all right…"

Kissing his face all over, digging his hands into his thick long hair, Steve was slow to control his urges. Without meaning to, he blurted out, "I am so in love with you!"

A rap at the door shocked them. They jumped apart as it opened. Mr. Parsons peeked in, smiling. "Just making sure there was no bloodshed."

Instantly Steve remembered he was to have told Mark about the Foist account.

"Oi?" Mark tilted his head curiously, trying to tame his hair.

"Are you all right, my boy?" Mr. Parsons asked Mark. "You're not upset, are you?"

"What?" Mark turned from one to the other. "What's going on?"

"I haven't had a chance to tell him, Harold. We got side-tracked." Steve felt as if he had lipstick on his face from their kiss, though that was absurd.

"Oh. I'm sorry, Steve. I'll let you continue. I do hope you two can remain friends after."

When Mr. Parsons left them alone, closing the door behind him, Mark said, "What the bloody hell is he on about?"

"Nothing. Look, when can we get together?"

Dropping down in his leather chair like a dead weight, Mark rested his head back on it and stared at Steve. "I don't bloody know."

"Do you love this woman?"

"I don't know anymore. I'm fed up with her at the moment. The woman has become a harpy. I can't breathe without her on me and yet she seems to be able to do as she pleases. Things are terrible between us, I'm afraid."

Steve moved across the room and knelt next to him, spinning the chair so he was between Mark's knees as he slouched back on the supple leather. "Because of me? Because of what happened?"

Mark rubbed his eyes tiredly.

"Mark!" Steve shook him, gripping both his thighs.

"Yes! All right? That's part of it. I'm trying to deal with these feelings I have for you as well. Being gay," Mark said, then lowered his voice. "Yes! But, it's worse than that."

"What's worse?" Steve began running his hands up and down those lovely legs.

"It's Jack."

Steve froze. "You said you and he—"

"No. We haven't. He's been in love with me since college, Steve. If he found out I went with another man it would crush him."

Completely stunned at the comment, Steve didn't know how to reply. Finally he breathed, "Jesus, Richfield, who doesn't love you?"

A sad laugh escaped Mark's throat.

"Don't tell Jack." Steve began rubbing those thighs again.

"Oh, bloody hell…what am I going to do?" he moaned.

"Please see me. Please…" Steve cupped both his palms over Mark's crotch. He was hard as a brick.

"You're hands are driving me mad."

At that line, Steve twisted back to the door, jumped up, locked it, then raced back to kneel in front of Mark.

"What are you doing? Are you completely insane?" Mark gasped as Steve went to open his slacks.

"Shut up and come, will ya?" Steve dove on his lap and stuffed that enormous cock down his throat. At first it felt absolutely bizarre to have a man's cock in his mouth, but that sensation was fleeting. Instantly the pleasure of making a man he was intensely in love with come was more stimulating than anything else he had experienced in his life. Dreaming of this kind of contact with him, Steve was giddy in the head over actually fulfilling this fantasy. Mark tasted divine, his scent was like an aphrodisiac, and his stifled grunts of euphoria were like a symphony to Steve's ears. Groaning in ecstasy, Steve wrapped his arms around Mark's narrow waist and pumped his hips into his mouth.

When he felt it ripple and heard Mark's stifled grunting, he swallowed him down in pleasure and then looked up to his face to judge the results.

Mark's hair was wild and covering his forehead. His head was tilted to the side and his eyes were shut with his lips opened to a breath. Setting back, staring at that large cock as it protruded from his designer clothing, Steve looked down at his own crotch and knew if Mark so much as touched him he would come. Slowly opening his eyes, Mark's green irises seemed misty and clouded. "You're completely insane," he whispered.

"Touch me. For Christ's sake, touch me!" Steve opened his trousers.

Looking around him to that closed door first, Mark sat up and reached down Steve's trousers. Oh, how long had he wanted to do this? Touch a man this way? Forever. Forever he had fought with what was in his heart. *Yes, I'm gay*! he shouted in his temples as if admitting what everyone had always accused him of. But, this time it was without shame. It was with pride. And what a man to touch! Mark used the back of his knuckles to caress Steve's cock first, lightly just so he wouldn't seem too eager, then he shouted in his head, *Oh, sod it*! and wrapped his fist around that shaft like he meant it. Hearing Steve's gasp was worth everything he owned. And the feel of his cock, that wonderful, perfectly shaped organ was enough to get him into a frenzied state. All he wanted to do was please him, give him that release, and feel the heat of the semen when it shot out.

Steve stared at Mark's naked cock, then came as Mark tried to contain the spill. Knowing they had to get decent before the next interruption, Steve stood up and tucked himself in. When he looked down, Mark was holding a palm-full of semen helplessly. At that sight, Steve burst out laughing.

"Oi! Help us out, will ya?" Mark shouted, then started laughing as well.

Steve looked around for something to wipe it with. He grabbed a piece of paper from the printer and handed it to him. Mark did his best to dispose of the mess, then looked down at his hands in dismay. "Should have swallowed," Steve grinned smugly.

"I have to close my trousers. My hands are a sticky mess. Give us a hand."

Steve tucked Mark's cock into his pants lovingly, then zipped and buttoned him up.

"Cheers. I have to go to the loo now to wash up. Open the door for us, would you?"

"Wait." Steve stopped him. "See me again. At home. Where we can roll around naked in the sheets."

"Oh, I'd love to...you know I would." Mark rubbed his hips against him hungrily.

"When?"

"Can I get back to you on that?"

"No. When?" Steve blocked his path.

It appeared Mark was trying to think of a day desperately. "I don't know...I don't know..."

"I need a date! Mark!"

"All right! Criminy, you cops are pushy. What day is today? Oh, yes, Monday. Uh..."

"Tonight?"

"No. Not tonight."

"Why not tonight? How about tomorrow then?"

"Tomorrow, tomorrow..."

"Tuesday!" Steve shouted, then tried to calm down.

"Yes. All right. Yes. Now let me wash up."

Steve opened the door for him. When they stepped out, Charlie was passing by and stopped short to look at them curiously. Then he reached out his hand to Steve and said, "Congratulations, Steve. Heard you got the Foist account."

Steve cringed and looked over at Mark's shocked

expression.

When he read the reactions, Charlie said, "Oops! Didn't Mark know? Sorry. I thought that cat was out of the bag." As he walked away he shrugged.

Steaming mad, Mark stormed down the hall to the men's toilet with Steve right behind him. "Mark! I was going to tell you! We got distracted!"

Mark held up his hand to silence him and checked the stalls first, then washed up at the sink, a steam cloud gathering around him. When he had dried his hands he turned around and said coldly, "Well, congratulations. I suppose the best man has won."

"Mark, cut it out. I don't want it. I want you to have it."

"I'm not bothered. Good luck to you."

"Mark! Mark, stop walking away." Steve chased him back down the hall then realized they were being spied by several other employees.

Finally Mark halted and hissed, "Stop humiliating me. Leave me to my work."

When he turned and stormed into his office, Steve clenched his fists in frustration and headed back to his desk. Sitting down, he rested his head in his hands and tried to think.

A short time later, Steve made his way to Mr. Parsons' office and knocked. He heard his *come in* and entered.

"Steve! Has Roland contacted you yet?"

"No...look, Harold, I've thought long and hard about this account and I think Richfield should get it."

"What? I don't understand, Steve. You've been working very hard for years and I just assumed the account would pass to you once Roland retired."

"Yes, so did I—originally. But, Richfield's really got what it takes to woo these people, Harold. Maybe my manner is too sharp, too blunt for the kind of clients they are. They're very rich, very upper class. Mark has all that. I'm just a bit too rough around the edges."

Blinking his eyes in surprise, Mr. Parsons finally

gestured for Steve to sit down. He did and felt as if the weight of the world was upon him.

"Steve...I'm not sure where this insecurity has come from. You have showed nothing but confidence and ability to me consistently. The idea that you aren't polished enough for this account is borderline preposterous. Has Mark made you feel guilty? Is that it?"

"No. No, Harold...I've got a lot on my plate and—"

"Nonsense! I want you to handle it. Enough said."

About to speak one line too many, Steve stopped himself, stood slowly and headed for the door. Before he left, Mr. Parsons said, "It's very noble of you, Steve, to consider Mark's feelings. But ultimately the decision is mine, and I have made it."

"Yes, sir." Steve attempted a weak smile, then left. He headed to the lounge for a cup of coffee. Several of his co-workers were there, all shouting congratulations and offering to shake his hand.

"I knew you would get it," David said. "You were awesome at the retreat, Steve. I think that's what tipped the scales."

Bret said, "You've been here, the one who worked towards it, it would have been really bad business to give it to the newcomer."

Kevin was about to add his commentary to the conversation when the door opened.

Stirring his milk into his coffee, Steve glanced up to see Mark coming in, looking completely devastated. The men shut up quickly and waited as he walked to a vending machine and bought a bottle of mineral water. It was agony not running to comfort him.

Bret cleared his throat in the awkward silence and said, "Hey, Mark, how's it going?"

"All right," Mark replied, "You?"

"All right," Bret nodded.

Seeing no one had anything else to say, Mark twisted the top off his bottle as he left the room.

"Mark..." Steve rushed after him, knowing behind him the suspicion and stares would be brutal.

Continuing to walk to his office, Mark replied flatly, "What?"

"Are we still on for Tuesday?"

A sarcastic laugh escaped Mark's throat.

Once again using his hands when his mouth failed him, Steve grabbed Mark at the elbow almost making him spill the water as he sipped it, and turned him around forcefully.

"Oi!" Mark shouted in protest.

"I have to speak to you...away from here. Please."

Rolling his eyes at the folly, Mark said, "I don't know what there is to say, but, fine! If it'll end this rubbish once and for all, fine!"

"Can you follow me home tonight? Just give me an hour...can you do that?"

"Let me make a phone call and I'll let you know."

Cringing, knowing that meant a call to "the fiancé", Steve released his grasp and nodded.

Though the pain of losing the account stung, Mark knew Steve was the better choice. It was all business and no hard feelings, right?

Sitting down at his desk, Mark picked up the phone for that obligatory call.

"Sharon?"

"What now?"

Mark paused and tried not to get annoyed. "I just wanted to say I'm going out with someone from work for a bit. I won't be home late."

"Maaark! Why? Why can't you just come home? I don't understand this. We're in the middle of the final plans for the wedding!"

"Sharon," Mark tried to calm her down but knew it was futile, "it's not going to take me long. Please. I'll be home and we can discuss whatever you need then."

"Oh, right! Just go out and forget about everything else!"

Covering his eyes, wishing he could end it right then and there, Mark inhaled a deep breath and said, "I haven't forgotten anything. I'll be home soon. Okay?"

After he hung up, he felt the sense of dread filling his belly. Even without Steve in the equation, this union just wasn't right. He felt it in his heart.

The TVR visible in his rear view mirror, Steve tried not to race over the roads to his home with the thought of Mark finally alone with him in his domain. He parked in his driveway while Mark pulled up on the street in front of his house. As he opened the door to his place, he twisted over his shoulder to see Mark approaching, his face expressing anger and disappointment. Steve assumed it was about the job.

"Come in." Steve held the door open for him and allowed him to pass.

Still holding his car keys, Mark stepped in, only as far as the foyer, and stopped. "Well? What do you have to say?"

"Cut it out, and get in here!" Steve grabbed his arm and once again brought him closer. "Take off your suit jacket and tie, and let me get us a beer."

With a big exhaled sigh of irritation, Mark removed his jacket as Steve did the same on his way to the kitchen. When he returned with two cold beers, he found Mark standing near a wall of photos. As if hearing him come in, Mark turned around and took the offered iced mug of ale. "Cheers," he said and tapped Steve's glass. Then after he took a sip, he pointed to Steve's academy class graduation photo. "How old were you when you joined?"

"Twenty-two. A mere baby." Steve looked over Mark's shoulder at it.

"Your dad's a cop as well?" Mark gestured to a family photo where Sgt. Dick Miller was in his uniform.

"He was. He's retired now." Steve touched Mark

shoulder and nodded his head for him to sit on the couch. Once they were both comfortable, Steve set his beer on a side table and faced Mark, leaning his arm on the back of the couch behind him. "Look, whether this can work or not, I don't know, but I just feel we need to talk some things over or I'll lose my mind."

"Welcome to my world." Mark laughed sadly.

"First of all, let me apologize for not telling you about the Foist account."

"Forget it."

"No. I won't forget it. Listen, I felt like shit about it and I didn't want to hurt your feelings."

"I understand."

"I have no idea why Harold gave it to me. You are much more suited for it, and I told him as much."

Mark spun around and met his eyes.

At the surprise in them, Steve nodded. "I did. I told him these people were too high class for me and you would be better suited for wooing them."

"You told him that?"

"Yes."

Facing forward once more, Mark sipped his beer as he appeared to digest the comment.

"Mark, I don't want to do anything that will hurt you. You have to believe me."

Softening slightly, Mark smiled at him and said, "I do, love."

"Good." Steve took a sip of his beer, then set it back down. "Now…about this 'fiancé' of yours…" Steve was unable to prevent his sneer.

Mark's smile vanished.

"When's the wedding?"

"Next month. August fifteenth."

"Shit. Are you kidding me?" Steve felt ill.

"No. I am not kidding you."

"Will you go through with it?"

"I don't know. I'm supposed to. It's all been planned."

Scooting over to him, Steve cupped the back of Mark's head with the hand he had resting on the back of the couch. Mark seemed to lavish in the touch. Steve reached for Mark's beer and set it next to his, then slowly he began to wrap around him and pull him close. Without the slightest struggle or hesitation, Mark complied and found his mouth.

Enjoying his taste and scent in ecstasy, Steve moaned in delirium at having him in his arms again. Their tongues teased each others'. Their hands coiled around each others' back and neck until their bodies were sealed together tightly. His head spinning, high on this man, Steve moaned, "I love you, oh, my baby, I love you so much." And as if Mark was lost on the passion as well, he whimpered a love-sick sound and allowed his head to fall back as Steve licked at his neck and jaw.

Pulling back abruptly, Steve panted, "Wait here…wait here…can you wait here?"

Blinking his eyes, as if coming around from a dream, Mark nodded, appearing slightly confused. Before Steve left the room, he said again, "Don't move."

"Yes…all right," Mark agreed quietly.

Racing to his bedroom, Steve dug through his closet, throwing things into the air in an effort to locate something.

A few minutes later he emerged. Seeing Mark sipping his beer calmly, Steve cleared his throat to get his attention. When Mark looked up, his expression was worth its weight in gold.

"Bloody hell…" Mark breathed in awe, his eyes wide.

"You like?" Steve grinned demonically.

"Bloody, bloody hell…" Mark sighed, standing up to move closer.

Steve looked down at his old uniform shirt and slacks. Even without the badge and gun belt, it seemed the effect was the same.

"You are one horny bloke, Officer Miller." Mark shook his head in admiration. "Oh, I'll bet the ladies all wanted a piece of you."

In a provocative gesture, Steve ran his hand down the front of his navy blue slacks and purred, "You want a piece of me?"

"Aye, I want more than a piece, love," Mark whispered.

With a wicked smile on his lips, Steve shoved Mark roughly and ordered, "Up against the wall!"

Immediately obeying, Mark placed his hands on the wall and waited.

"Spread 'em," Steve nudged his feet with his shoe until Mark's legs were wide apart.

"I didn't do it, copper," Mark teased.

"That's what they all say." Steve leaned one of his legs against Mark's inner thigh, then began at his fingers and started smoothing his hands down his arms to his shoulders. He reached under Mark's hair to his neck, feeling inside his shirt collar, then slid them down his sides to his waistband.

"Oh, bloody hell..." Mark whispered excitedly. "I'm going to spurt, love..."

Leaning his shoulder on Mark's back, very slowly, Steve moved his hands to Mark's pelvis, running his fingers down the front of Mark's trousers very close to his zipper and the hard cock underneath. Mark began fidgeting in excitement. Steve lowered to Mark's wide muscular thighs, smoothing down them with both hands, rubbing inside his legs and under his balls.

"Oh, flamin' hell! Jesus, Steve!" Mark looked down at Steve's hands, panting to catch his breath.

Methodically, Steve moved to the next leg, doing the same, squeezing and smoothing his hands down to Mark's calf. Then he used his right hand to rub between Mark's legs, reaching through them to cup his cock from behind.

Arching his back, Mark pushed his hips forward, into Steve's hot hand and began humping it, grunting, yearning for the friction.

Behind him Steve was in the same state. His heart rate was soaring, his respiration was climbing to a panting gasp. With his right hand still between Mark's legs, he used his left to smooth up Mark's tight abdomen and chest, all the while rubbing his face against Mark's back and neck. In a wild movement, Mark spun around and grabbed Steve's face, sucking at his mouth and tongue, then he jumped up and wrapped his legs around Steve's waist, pushing his cock into his pelvis and whimpering in agony for satisfaction.

With Mark attached to him, Steve carried him to his bedroom, still kissing him passionately, unwilling to release either his mouth or his hold on his body.

Finally, Mark parted for breath and gasped, "Fuck me...fuck me..."

"Oh, yes..." Steve laughed wickedly, and set him down on the bed with a bounce. Before Steve could take off his clothing, Mark stopped him.

"No...don't take that off."

Grinning demonically, Steve nodded, then went about stripping Mark of his business suit. Once Mark was naked and splayed out on his bed, Steve paused and stared down at him. "Look at you..." he breathed, shaking his head. "Christ, you are fantastic."

"Shut up and shag me..." Mark reached out for him, spreading his legs in invitation.

Finding the package of lubrication and the condom he had bought in hopes of this occasion, Steve made a show of coating himself with it after putting on the rubber, then climbed over the bed to a very eager Mark.

Taking a moment to stare at him first, Steve moved his slippery fingers around Mark's heavy balls to his anus. Imagining what penetrating him would feel like, he slipped one finger inside him, as if to see what his reaction would be. Mark inhaled in a hiss and arched his back. "Nice?" Steve asked softly.

"Oh, god yes...holy Christ."

The rush of blood to his cock at that comment was amazing. Steve imagined jamming his hips into him ruthlessly, but was aware that this was all new to Mark as well. Two fingers made their way in.

G.A. Hauser

Mark gasped and asked in a breathy voice, "Please, love…take it."

Adjusting his position on the bed, Steve set himself on target. When he pushed into a male body for the first time he felt his brain melt. The pleasure of connecting to Mark that way, so intimate and personal, was as if he'd been a virgin all his life and this was his first taste of real sex.

About to ask Mark if he was all right, he felt him pushing his hips back, making Steve go deeper inside. "Wow," Steve said without realizing it. "That good?" he asked.

"Oh, my god…"

"Wow!" Steve gripped Mark with more confidence and began humping this gorgeous pretty boy with new found zeal. Mark was becoming very vocal underneath him, holding his legs at the knees to keep his thighs open. Steve loved being able to see his face the entire time. His vision kept bouncing from Mark's gorgeous face, to his fantastic set of male anatomy. Wanting to satisfy Mark as well, Steve tried to get a good grip on his cock and keep up his momentum at the same time.

Mark had never felt anything like it. It was as if a light had been flicked on and he wished all those years of denying he was gay would vanish. Why on earth did he fight this? Nothing compared to it.

Opening his eyes, seeing that fantastic cop, big, macho, and devilishly handsome, thrusting his hips into him that way, was such a fantasy he didn't need Steve to touch him, but oh, he was glad he did.

Getting right on the edge of an orgasm, Steve closed his eyes in reflex and shivered. He pumped deep and slow until he was awash with chills. He opened his eyes and looked at Mark's face. Mark was staring at him, his mouth open, his

84

eyes wild, his hair an unruly mane of brown. Thrusting in quickly, Steve came, clenching his jaw and shivering from head to toe.

"You lovely fucker," Mark whispered sensuously, "You absolutely lovely fucker…"

Steve pulled out, dropped the spent condom onto the floor, then crouched down on Mark to suck him. Arching his back from the intensity, Mark gripped the bed and rocked with it, gasping out loud and reeling from the aftershocks.

Once they had recuperated, Steve managed to shed the uniform and cuddle up around Mark on the bed. As they rested and listened to each other's breathing slow down to a normal rate, Steve whispered, "You are amazing."

"Me?" Mark laughed at the absurdity.

"Yes, you." Steve squeezed him closer.

"I've never felt anything quite that intense. What is it about you?"

"I love you, that's what it is. I swear, Mark, I have never been this head over heels in love with anyone before."

"I am so flattered, Steve. Flattered beyond words." He kissed Steve's forehead.

"Do…do you feel anything for me?" Steve asked timidly.

"Oh, yes…make no mistake." Mark hugged him tight.

"Then…then what will you do?"

"Do?"

Steve sat up and looked down at Mark in the dimness of the room. "Do. You know… About this wedding thing."

When Mark's eyes darted away, Steve exhaled and rested his head back on his chest. He wanted this man in his bed every night. How the hell were they supposed to accomplish that?

After a long moment of lying quietly intertwined on top of the sheets, Mark began talking in a low soft whisper. "I suppose this was bound to happen…it seemed everyone around me has always suspected me of being gay and I was the last to admit it."

Steve kept quiet and nestled into his hair for a sniff and to offer some comfort.

Sighing, Mark continued, "I've been accused of it all me life, really. Ever since I was a young lad my father shouted rude things at me, said I was too soft, too mothered. Then when I got a bit older, he hit me and called me a faggot all the time. We got into quite a battle over that same topic the day he had a stroke. He died soon after. Well, then there's Jack. He may have suspected I was gay as well. The minute we met I have to admit there was attraction between us. But I never allowed us to touch that way. I suppose I had to prove everyone wrong. It was as if there was a principle involved." Smiling to himself for a brief moment, Mark then whispered, "I remember one night we got drunk in our dorm room. He really tried to convince me we should have sex. Used every excuse in the book, he did. I refused. I think I broke his heart that night."

"College?" Steve asked. "I thought you were from England? How did you go to college together?"

"I was born in England but moved here when I was a young boy. Jack and I met at Stamford whilst playing baseball."

"Oh. Sorry, go on." Steve snuggled back into his hair again.

After a deep inhale of breath, Mark said, "Well, the ironic thing was this relationship with Sharon...she assumed Jack and I were lovers as well and constantly confronted me over it. I, of course, kept denying it, because, well, quite frankly we weren't. But, I was getting sick to death of everyone accusing me of it. Ages ago, when I was first starting out, working as an architect for a small firm in east LA, I was even harassed about it. Someone kept leaving gay porno magazines on my desk. I quit after that. Jack was so furious he wanted me to sue, but I didn't want the fuss and publicity."

"Jesus, Mark..." Steve hugged him closer.

"I could go on and on, Steve, about the rubbish I endured, but, why bother. And the greatest irony of all? Here I am, in a man's bed, so sexually satisfied I could cry. So? After all the denying, the fighting, the mental anguish, I am exactly where everyone thought I was. But, love, where do I go from here?"

"You end the heterosexual relationship you don't really want and you come and live here with me."

Smiling sadly, Mark replied, "Like that is an easy solution? Are you joking?"

"No. I'm dead serious." Steve sat up and brushed Mark's hair back from his face.

"I'd destroy so many people on so many levels. How selfish would that be?"

Gripping Mark's hands in his, Steve said, "Mark, if we don't stay together we'll be completely miserable. How stupid would that be?" he mimicked.

"But, my dearest, closest companions would be crushed. Think of what this would do to Sharon. She had a devil of a time convincing her father I wasn't bi. And then Jack…poor Jack would be so jealous and upset he'd never speak to me again."

"I'm sorry about all this, Mark. I wish I could prevent my feelings for you. But I can't. Is there anything I can do to help out? Talk to Jack? Do something to help you out of the mess I've helped create?" When Mark rested back on the pillows and closed his eyes, Steve cuddled once more next to him and sighed, "Look, you're not the only one who's had a rough time." Once Mark opened his eyes to acknowledge him, Steve said, "I said my father retired from the police, but that's not really the truth…he was forced out when he threatened me and my last girlfriend with a gun."

"Wha-at?" Mark gasped.

"You heard me. I dated a black attorney and he went ballistic."

"That's unbelievable."

"He was on duty, in his fricken' uniform, when Sonja

and I stopped for a coffee at a Starbucks. He spotted us kissing and made a public spectacle of himself."

"Crikey."

"They took his badge away from him after that. I have to admit, I quit soon after they let him go. Sonja constantly complained about me working on the streets. She was deathly afraid I'd get killed."

"I can understand that." Mark caressed Steve's face lovingly.

"Well, I finally gave into her pressure and started working at the bottom rung at Parsons & Company."

"Why did you two split up?"

Trying not to show his pain over it, Steve stared at the shadows on the wall of the bedroom when he said, "I don't know…I think she just got bored of me. The sex was great, but we didn't have anything in common."

A wry smile played across Mark's lips.

Once Steve noticed it he nudged him. "What?"

"It sounds familiar."

"Stop it. We have everything in common."

"Do we?"

"Yes! Our jobs, our fathers, our enjoyment of being physically fit…loads of things."

"But, working together in the same office and having a relationship? That isn't sensible."

"We hardly see each other in that office. We're always out on the road. Don't even play that game."

Mark checked the time on the digital clock by the bed, then sighed and tried to relax once more. In the dimness of the room, Steve stared at his profile. "You have to go?"

"Yes, but I don't want to."

"Stay."

Mark laughed softly.

Just as Steve was about to say something, the sound of a ring-tone was heard muffled in the room.

"Bullocks," Mark muttered, and tried to sit up and get off the bed.

Releasing him from their embrace, Steve watched as Mark dug around his suit jacket pockets and answered his mobile phone.

"Yes... No, I'm all right... No, I'm not with Sharon..." Mark quickly glanced at Steve who was listening intently. "Uh...I'm still in the office. I know it's late. It just took longer than I expected... Look, Jack, just forget dinner for me...I'll catch something here... When? I don't know...does it matter? Don't use that tone with me, Larsen..."

Steve smiled sadly.

"I have to go, Jack... Yes. No, I don't bloody know! You already treat me like a flamin' wife, for pity's sake! No, I'm not angry with you, but you are trying my patience at the moment...yes, he's here too... Why? Why should it make a difference who is here in the office with me?"

Steve covered his smile. So, Jack was already jealous of him?

"I've got to get back to work, Jack, let me go...bye." Mark hung up and shut the phone off.

Once he dropped it into his pocket and climbed back on the bed, Steve wrapped around him again and stared at him. "You okay?"

"No. I'm not bloody okay. I just had to lie to him. It's as if he already knows we're shagging."

"Smart man." Steve coiled around Mark and reached between his legs for a feel.

"Yes, he's very smart."

"Mmm..." Steve massaged Mark's soft cock and balls affectionately, nuzzling into his neck and licking his earlobe.

Closing his eyes, Mark spread his legs and whispered, "Very smart indeed."

"Christ, you have a big dick," Steve whispered, smoothing his palm along its hardened length.

"So, I've heard." Mark's hips began to come alive, rising and falling in time with the stroking.

"What a body you have…" Steve sucked in a breath of air through his teeth, "What an amazing body…narrow hips, flat solid stomach, tight buns, ooohhh, Mark, you are perfect, fucking perfect…"

"Look who's talking?" Mark laughed softly.

Steve climbed over Mark's legs to straddle him and sat up, looking down at him. "But, it's your face that's the most amazing. I can't get over what you look like."

"Looks are skin deep, love. Under this skin, I'm a bloody mess."

"Everyone is a bloody mess without skin!" Steve teased.

"You know what I mean, love. Me head is such a muddle."

Bracing his arms on the bed on either side of Mark, Steve began rubbing his own cock against the one under him. "Forget the crap in your head for a few minutes and let's get lost on each other again."

"Yes, all right, love…molest me…do naughty things to me."

A chill rushed up Steve's spine. "Oh?"

Mark reached his arms out to the sides of the bed. "Tie me up, tie me down."

"Growl!" Steve wiggled in excitement.

"You still have your handcuffs?"

Steve burst out laughing, "Shut up…you can't be serious."

"I am. With you I am. I want to be at your mercy, your slave."

"Jesus, Mark!" Steve shivered in anticipation. "Don't even tease me like that!"

"Be rough on me…fuck me raw."

Blinking his eyes at his expression, trying to decide if this was just a trick to excite him beyond his wildest dreams, Steve felt his cock throb so hard it was almost painful. "You sure, Mark? I mean, I just did it to you a minute ago and that was your first time, right? So no, babe, next time I'll fuck you raw. Okay? But, we can still play."

90

He fell down on Mark and gripped his wrists, as if forcing him to stay pinned back, then found his mouth and sucked on it hotly, his head spinning. With his weight on top of him, Steve rubbed his cock against Mark's pubic hair and thighs, yearning to penetrate him and spurt come all over him at the same time.

As if somehow the act would rid the emotional wreck in his brain, Mark begged him. "Take me, Steve, take what you will...I'm yours, I'm yours..."

Overwhelmed by the sexual teasing talk, the look of submission on Mark's face, and his pliable positions, Steve whimpered in torment. "Stop...I can't handle it...stop...it makes me want to devour you."

Moving out of his grip, Mark rolled to his stomach and spread his legs, raising his perfect bottom into the air. Steve could only gape in awe. With fumbling fingers, he stared at the lubrication as it sat on the nightstand but didn't reach for it, waiting to see if this was really what Mark wanted. Kneeling behind Mark, seeing his completely subservient posture, hands stretched out, legs wide, he could barely function. When Mark hissed, "Take it, baby," Steve grabbed his hips in both hands and wanted to push in, shivering as if a cold sweat had enveloped him. "No, Mark, it's too soon after the first one." Steve breathed.

"Fuck me, lover, fuck me raw..." Mark whimpered as if he was lost.

With that lovely cooing accent encouraging him, Steve crushed him into his arms and rocked him. And as if knowing Steve would not be rough on him or hurt him, Mark spun around and grabbed Steve's cock in his hands. The sensations of chills were so intense Steve thought his cock would blow off when he came. Mark appeared determined to give him another amazing orgasm. Splayed

91

out on the bed, his legs wide as this adorable man did his best to please him, when Mark dove onto Steve's pelvis and sucked hard on him, Steve felt chills rush up his spine to the tip of his cock. In reflex, he shoved into Mark's mouth harder, and grunted a deep masculine sound as Mark echoed it. Slowly coming around, Steve didn't want to take his cock out of Mark's mouth as the aftershocks continued to rock his body. Staring down at the sight of Mark still lapping at his cock gently, he truly felt as if he couldn't get enough of him. When Mark finally sat back, looking down at him, Steve stared at that lovely expression and then his unsatisfied cock. Knowing it was his turn to be there for his lover, he reached for the lube and rubbers once more. Trying not to feel nervous about his first time being penetrated, Steve thought only of Mark. Making him happy, making him whole, and satisfying him. Very gently, he applied a rubber, then lube to Mark's cock making him slick with it. Getting to his hands and knees, Steve looked over his shoulder as Mark knelt up behind him.

Mark stared at the lovely tight rounded bottom of Steve's ass. *This is it*, he thought, *this act confirms everyone's suspicions about you, Richfield.*

"Oh, piss off," he mumbled, as if telling all those invisible critics to shut up. It was so low Steve didn't hear it. Getting himself on target, he asked, "You ready, copper?"

"It seemed to go over well with you, so? Go for it."

Mark smiled. "Oh, you'll like it, I promise." He held onto Steve's hips and pushed in gently. "You still okay, Officer Miller?"

"Ten-four."

Mark chuckled, then penetrated until he was all the way in. He heard a luscious groan from Steve and knew very well what that felt like. Still moving with care, Mark started rocking and allowed it to build up slowly.

Steve loved it! He never imagined it was going to be so amazing. And the thought of it being Mark, Mark's cock, Mark's body, that was enough to make him completely overwhelmed. "Oh, Richfield, I adore you."

As if it was what Mark was waiting to hear, Steve felt him thrust in with more confidence. Hearing Mark's orgasmic masculine grunt, Steve felt his cock throbbing and smiled in complete pleasure.

After what felt like frenzied activity, Mark disengaged himself from Steve, disposed of the rubber to the pile on the floor, then sat back to stare at him.

A demonic smile had played on that gorgeous man's lips. Steve's brain spinning with the amazing sensations, he shook his head in awe and whispered, "I have got to get you into my life permanently."

And with tacit approval, Mark just smiled back wickedly.

Chapter Ten

It was impossible to pretend they weren't wildly attracted to each other. Passing in the corridor, both hiding their sly smiles, Steve enjoyed the perception that they still hated, or barely tolerated each other, while they kept their secret hidden. A new sign was installed on Steve's office door, "Vice President of Media Operations". He barely noticed it, and didn't care what it read. As far as he was concerned it could have read "Richfield's Bitch" and he would be happy.

Mark's fingers ran over the keyboard of the computer as if he were playing a concerto on a baby grand, his focus completely on his work. When he heard her voice, he jolted in surprise. "Sharon?"

"Hey…I just thought I'd stop by. Typically, you never invited me to see your office." She walked in, looking around the large room curiously. "A bit small, isn't it?"

Instantly Mark regretted her visit, thinking of what Steve may or may not do when he spotted her. "You shouldn't have come unannounced, Sharon. I may have been out of the office. I'm not here at my desk very much."

"Gee thanks! I'm so glad I bothered!" She set her purse down on the leather chair opposite him. "Don't I get a proper kiss hello?"

Feeling awkward suddenly, Mark stood and walked

around the desk, pecking her cheek lightly. The last thing he wanted was for Steve to witness any of this. He knew it would upset him. "Look, I am busy, Sharon..."

"You're always busy, that's the problem. I just wondered if you were picking me up on the way to the club tonight, or if you'll meet us there."

The room feeling hot suddenly, Mark remembered his plans with Steve and tried to loosen his collar with his index finger, tugging at it uncomfortably. "...I can't tonight, sorry..."

"Why not, Mark?" she whined in that way that he detested. It was nasally and high–pitched, like a toddler. "Mom and Dad are expecting us! I told them we would be there for dinner!" She looked down her nose coldly at him.

Feeling annoyed at her possessive attitude, he replied, "You told them that before you asked if I was busy."

"You know, you're really starting to piss me off. What's the damn deal? What are you doing that's so important you can't come to the club for a meal?" She crossed her arms over her chest. "Mark, the wedding is coming up and it would be nice if you were involved in the last few details of it. You know, Mom, Katie, and I have been doing it all on our own. You need to be there as well! I want you to be doing all these things and not leaving it all to me..."

His temper began to rise at the pressure he was feeling, her non-stop whining, and her constant need to control him. He sighed, "What could I contribute, Sharon? You need money? You know my checkbook is open. Just tell me how much."

"No, not just money, Mark! What's going on? Suddenly it's as if you've gone cold on me. It's not Jack, is it? If it is, I'll scream! I can't take much more of this pressure! Everything is on me! Me, me, me!"

"Yes, it's always been about you, Sharon, I know." He tried not to roll his eyes. "Oh, and don't start on me about Jack again," Mark replied, throwing up his hands in frustration. "Always blaming Jack for our difficulties. It's really not fair, Sharon. The poor man does nothing to deserve it. If you need someone to blame, blame me. Not Jack. Our problems are between us. No one else."

"Then what's going on? Are you reconsidering our marriage? Mark, if you have any reservations, tell me now."

On a trip to the men's room, Steve was about to poke his head in and smile at him when he noticed a blonde, very well dressed woman in Mark's office. Instantly on guard, Steve paused to listen unnoticed at the office door.

Mark had his opportunity to come clean, and he wanted to with every bone in his body. Ever since he had proposed he felt it was a mistake. And now that he had fallen hard for his co-worker, he knew he could never go through with it. But the plans this woman had made, her time, effort, and care in making this the most important day of her life was weighing on him heavily. Could he break her heart like that? Or should he continue pretending he was not in love with a man? It was making him so miserable, he felt as if he needed to cry at the injustice and could only blame himself.

Sighing, feeling like the worst kind of heel, he whispered, "No, no, love, don't worry…everything is all right. Don't upset yourself. Tell Daddy-Teddy I'll be there."

"Thank you, Mark. You know what he's like. I just as soon keep him off my back."

"Yes. Yes, I know." Mark despised the man, and even the thought of having that bully and homophobe as a father-in-law made him cringe in disgust.

She turned around quickly as if she sensed someone behind her.

Mark looked around her to see who had come in. "Steve?" He died inside, then wondered how much he had overheard of their conversation.

Unable to back out now, Steve smiled quickly to cover his agony and held out his hand to her. "You must be the lucky lady."

She brightened instantly and shook his hand. "That's what they tell me."

Clearing his throat in anxiety, Mark introduced them.

When Steve stood back to judge her appearance, it seemed as if she was doing the same thing to him. If she knew Mark at all, then she had reasons to suspect him right from the start. But how well did she know him?

In the awkwardness of the meeting, Mark said, "Steve used to be an LAPD cop. Doesn't he still resemble one?"

"Oh?" She looked from Mark back to Steve skeptically.

"Mark has a thing for cops," Steve said, intentionally causing suspicion, "He keeps calling me Officer Miller."

Instantly Mark's face went beet red.

"Do you?" The bug of suspicion immediately bit her.

"Uh...aren't you busy, Steve?" Mark made an anxious face at him, trying to give him a hint to leave.

"No. Are you two going to have lunch together? I'd love to join you."

Before Mark could protest, Sharon was accepting his invitation. Reading her face easily, Steve could well imagine the thoughts in her head. Know your competition? Keep your enemies close? Either one would do.

"I'll just hit the men's room and be right back," Steve said, pointing down the hall.

"Uh, yes. Me too." Mark nudged Sharon aside and avoided her look of mistrust. "Be right back, love."

The minute they were down the hall, Mark started shoving Steve to hurry. Once they were in the men's room and Mark looked into all the stalls to make sure they were empty, he shouted. "What the bloody hell do you think you're doing?"

Innocently Steve replied, "She seems nice. I just thought I'd get to know her." He unzipped his pants while still facing Mark, then after showing him his cock, he turned to relieve himself in the urinal.

And staring directly at the lewd act, Mark became distracted, then stood at the next one and opened his pants to pee.

After he had finished, Steve stared at Mark's cock overtly. "What a dick you have, Richfield."

"Stop this nonsense at work." Mark quickly completed the task of zipping up, then went to the sink to wash his hands as Steve did the same. "I know why you invited yourself, and I'm not well pleased."

"I just want to see if she's good enough for you."

"It's not up to you to judge!" Mark shouted through clenched teeth.

Moving behind him, Steve wrapped around his waist and rubbed his hips into Mark's, looking at them both in the mirror's reflection. "Stop worrying, baby."

Instantly aroused, Mark closed his eyes and leaned back against Steve's hard body. The doubts in his mind swirled around him like ghosts at a séance. When Steve started kissing his neck under his hair, Mark was getting the feeling that fighting this attraction was useless. Those large masculine hands moved down his chest to his crotch. Opening his eyes a crack, Mark could see them both in the mirror, Steve nuzzling into his hair, his fingers tracing the length of his cock through his slacks. All he wanted to do was spin around, suck on his mouth, and then get to his knees and rip open his zipper. "It's useless," Mark sighed tiredly, as if admitting to himself that trying to prevent fate was possible.

At a noise at the door, Mark shoved him back and straightened his suit jacket in the mirror anxiously. "We need to be careful!"

"I know," Steve responded quietly.

When they stepped out of the toilet she was there, arms

crossed, her expression so pinched it was as if the men could read her betrayal even before she could realize she had been deceived.

Steve opened the door for her and allowed her to pass out of the office and into the hall. As they stood at the elevators quietly, Mark deliberately didn't look at Sharon's angry glare. When it opened they stepped back to allow a few people off, then entered it and pushed the button for the garage floor.

With his back towards Steve, Mark tried to compose himself and get his thoughts straight. When someone reached for his bottom and gave it a nice caress, he stiffened slightly but didn't react, knowing it must be Steve. As if Sharon felt the invisible electricity, she tilted over her shoulder and looked down, deliberately as if she were checking for the contact she had just missed. Steve shook his head sadly as if wondering why this woman wanted to enter into a committed relationship with a man who had a sexuality question mark so pronounced on his head. Mark felt another grope to his bottom. In complete irony, he spun around and shot a very accusatory glare at Steve for the caress. In tacit denial, Steve tilted his head in a gesture for Mark to look at whose hand it was. When he realized it was Sharon's he went pale. The entire communication was not lost on her. The moment they stepped out of the elevator and into the parking garage she stopped them both and crossed her arms over her chest. "Okay, what the hell's going on?"

Immediately Mark shouted back defensively, "Nothing! Stop accusing me of this rubbish!"

With sick amusement, Steve kept mute and observed.

"Marrrrk," she whined, "Tell me what's going on between you guys!"

"Nothing! Sharon, stop this instant!" The blush was hot on his face as he tried to decide how to deal with an issue that was growing bigger by the moment.

"Steve?" She focused on him, as if he would be more

honest than her own beloved fiancé.

"Moi?" he replied innocently, pressing his hand to his chest. "I'm starved. Where do you want to go for lunch?" He removed his car keys from his pocket and made a move to his car. "I'll drive."

After she shot a very dirty look at Mark, she walked over to the Mercedes and stood at the front passenger door, obviously indicating she would ride shot-gun and Mark would be exiled to the back seat.

Once again when they were confined inside the car, she leaned over to Mark and asked, "You screwed each other? Does Jack know?"

Steve cringed as Mark let out a very loud sound in protest, as if he were passing a kidney stone. "Augh! I cannot deal with this, Sharon! Why are you marrying me if you believe I am shagging men? I am tired of it, you hear me? Why do I always have to defend my sexuality to you? Do you have any idea how annoying this has become?"

"Because!" she shouted, "You think I'm an idiot and can't tell when you are screwing someone! I'm not an idiot, Mark."

"Wow." Steve muttered, "Uh...lunch?" He started the car.

Leaning forward over the back of the seat to her, Mark argued, "Look, Sharon, simply because Steve is a handsome, virile man does not mean—"

"Wow again! Thanks, Mark," Steve interrupted, then caught both their angry eyes and shut up.

"Just tell me!" Sharon insisted.

"We are not having an affair!" Mark replied, but he kept wondering if he should just tell her and get this disaster over with. Even though it felt like the right thing to do, he held back, as if he needed time to make such a monumental decision.

"Right. Whatever." She crossed her arms defensively and sat facing the front.

"Ah, does salad sound good? I know a nice place." Steve

put it into reverse and backed out of the space.

"Sharon, listen to me," Mark pleaded, and felt as if he needed to keep his sanity for a moment. "Steve just got a large account to deal with. He has asked me to help him with it. It's huge and it's a massive responsibility. I have offered to give him a hand to get it organized. Ask him. Steve, tell Sharon."

"I did just get a promotion. And I do need Mark's help." He stopped at the gate and used his pass to open it, then headed out into the bustling traffic of downtown LA.

"There, you see?" Mark gestured. "Really, Sharon, you think every time I am seen with a handsome male I am sticking my dick in him."

Steve peered down at his lap nervously.

"I'm sorry, Mark. It was just that in the elevator when I touched your ass you turned and looked back at Steve to see if he had done it. I mean, come on."

"Sharon, Steve is a bit of a rascal. He does things because he thinks he'll get a reaction." With his arms dangling over the back seat, he could smell a trace of Steve's cologne and to him it was much more enticing than Sharon's sweet perfume.

"Do I?" Steve laughed, then found Mark's eyes in the rear view mirror. Smiling at him, Steve then asked Sharon nervously, "What are you looking at?"

At the comment, Mark sat up in panic and tried to see her face. She was deliberately staring at Steve's lap as if she were looking for some sign he was turned on.

"Nothing," she breathed tiredly, then muttered, "Nice hard-on."

His face rushing with his blush, Steve cleared his throat and said, "Well, you are very pretty."

"Yeah, right." She shook her head and stared out of the window dully.

In the back seat, Mark rubbed his face in exhaustion and mumbled, "Oh, bullocks..."

They were escorted to a sunny outdoor table with an

umbrella fending off the burning glare. After they sat down and ordered drinks, Steve loosened his tie and removed his jacket to hang over the seat, then rolled up his sleeves.

Sharon stared at him and said bitterly, "He's got the same fricken build as Jack."

"No way," Steve shook his head. "Jack's much bigger than I am."

Mark's face went ashen as he shot Steve a reprimanding look.

Then Sharon asked dryly, "Oh? Already met Jack? And when did that happen?"

Throwing up his hands in frustration, Steve answered, "Look, lady, if you can't trust the guy, why the hell are you marrying him? Jesus…"

"Steve!" Mark admonished, getting a sense that he was a sinking ship.

"Good question," Sharon sneered.

The drinks were set down in front of them, and downed quickly in the stressful situation.

His head drooping into his hands, Mark felt as if he were losing it. A debate began raging in his head, *Tell her! Don't tell her!* and he just didn't know the correct way to deal with it.

"What does Jack think of the two of you being so close?" she sneered.

Mark knew she was trying to use Jack as some kind of leverage in her argument. And unfortunately, dealing with Jack's feelings, if and when he found out about Steve, was something he was trying not to think about. Sighing tiredly, Mark just replied, "Please stop this, Sharon."

"Why the hell would Jack care?" Steve asked, looking back at Mark curiously. "They're not lovers."

"Steve, keep well clear of this, please," Mark said, trying to make his opinion obvious.

Sharon replied back to Steve, "No, supposedly they're not, but he's closer to Jack than any other human being."

"And you're okay with that?" Steve choked in shock.

Sharon replied, "I've come to terms with a lot of things concerning Mark."

"I don't know if that's liberal of you, or completely naïve."

"Steve..." Mark shot Steve another admonishing glare. "You think you're helping matters?"

"What?" Steve shrugged. "You don't think it's weird to be closer to your damn roommate than your fiancé and you don't even screw him?"

"Be quiet," Mark snapped at him.

Steve finished his Corona and asked, "Are you marrying him for his money or his big dick?"

"Steve!" Mark whacked his shoulder in fury and looked back at Sharon in panic.

All Sharon did was sneer in anger at the reaction. Finally she said, "How the hell do you know he's got a big dick?"

"You know the two of you are starting to really get on me nerves..." Mark warned.

It appeared to Mark as if Steve was about to say something witty about his anatomy, when the waiter finally asked if they were ready. Thankful for the interruption, Mark ordered some food and then handed him the menu. After the man left, Mark said, "Can we please move on to another topic?"

"So," Sharon began, waving her hand at Mark as if to disregard him, "What was it like being a cop in LA?"

"Insane. My ex-girlfriend couldn't handle it."

"Ex-girlfriend?" Sharon asked.

"Yessss?" Steve grinned slyly at her.

"Nothing. So, she didn't like you out there in a patrol car, huh?"

"No. Couldn't stand it. She nagged me constantly about quitting."

"Is that why you broke up?"

"No. Forget that. What do you do?"

Looking from one to the other, Mark was beginning to feel as if he were at a tennis match. He knew Steve was digging at her, trying to find her Achilles' heel so he could compete.

"I work with my father."

Steve glanced at Mark quickly to see his face, then answered sarcastically, "Daddy's little executive?"

Mark kicked Steve under the table, and in response he got a wicked smile.

"Yes." Sharon sat up as if she were proud of the title. "So? What of it? I don't mind working for him."

"Oh, I'm sure it was the easy route." Steve shook his head and sipped his drink.

"All right," Mark admonished. "Please let's not allow this to deteriorate again. Can't we be pleasant?"

Before their meal was served Sharon excused herself to go to the ladies room.

Once she had left, Mark met Steve's eyes wearily. "Why did you come with us? You know this is really unbelievable behavior."

"Don't be upset."

Rolling his eyes at the folly, Mark replied, "Look, whether or not Sharon and I get on with this wedding is between us. I really resent you harassing her."

Scooting his chair closer, Steve rubbed his thigh in comfort. "I'm not harassing her. And you worry too much."

"Do I? Come on, Steve. You are stirring it up. Please, allow me to make the decisions where Sharon is concerned."

"Why? You'll go through with it simply to spare her feelings or because they have already planned it. I've seen it happen that way before. Weddings are like steam rollers, people feel they can't be stopped once they have momentum." Steve ran his hand back through Mark's hair, getting it away from his face so he could see his eyes.

Knowing that was partly true, Mark exhaled a deep breath. "Yes, in some ways. But, if I feel this wedding shouldn't occur, it won't. Believe me, Steve, I'm going to have a lot to think about in the near future."

"Ohh, my poor baby," Steve cooed and cupped his jaw.

"Uh, Steven?" Mark peeked around the patio nervously.

"Yes, gorgeous?"

"People are watching."

"Oh?" Steve smiled wickedly.

"No, don't you dare!" Mark was just about to pull back when Steve kissed his lips. After he parted from him he heard a few giggles in the background.

"Wow..." Steve laughed, "That was liberating!" Then he looked around and said, "Shit, I should have made sure my old man wasn't around. He'd have shot me for that one."

Blinking his eyes at him in complete amazement, Mark sighed, "Why don't you just bloody up and tell her! You've done everything but!"

"It's your place to tell her. Not mine."

"Yes! And you remember that, will you?" Mark shouted, then looked up and found her there.

"Tell me what?" she asked, her bad attitude showing like a mask as she set her purse down and sat in the seat again.

"Nothing." Mark sat upright in his seat and looked to see if the waiter was coming with their food, shivering in fear that she may have spied their kiss.

Mark noticed when she met Steve's eyes for an answer, he looked away from her intelligent gaze quickly. Sickened by the lies and looking to the future with dread, Mark had completely lost his appetite and knew he had to make some decisions.

Leaving Mark to walk her to her car, Steve rode the elevator to the top floor and knew he had to get some work done. This thing with Mark was a distraction, to say the least. Just the thought of Mark marrying that woman was enough to bring his blood to a boil and his teeth clenching. And feeling as if he couldn't do or say anything to influence that decision just made him angry.

It was as if they were back to square one. Hating each

other.

Chapter Eleven

Knowing Mark would never answer a call from him over the weekend when he was most likely with Sharon, Steve let his obsession go temporarily and tried to get on with his normal routine. Tying his house key onto his sneaker lace, he stretched out a little first, then began his run in the cool breezy morning before the sun burned too brightly and the heat became unbearable. Moving at a quick but comfortable pace, he heard the honk of a horn and at first he jumped back thinking he was in someone's way. He then realized the person inside the vehicle was waving at him.

"Holy shit," Steve breathed in amazement, and stopped running as the maroon Jaguar pulled up next to him on the street. Panting to catch his breath, he leaned into the passenger side as the window lowered down. "Jack Larsen, what the hell are you doing up so early?"

"Just coming back from getting the paper and some bagels for breakfast. You look great. How far do you run?"

"On a good day, five or so. Just depends how I feel." He wiped the sweat off his face as it dripped down.

"Why don't you stop by after your workout? You free?"

"Yeah...okay...uh, what's Mark up to?"

"Some crap he had to do with Sharon. Wedding preparation or something. I don't ask anymore."

"All right. Give me an hour or so."

"Great, see ya then...oh, bring a bathing suit."

Nodding, Steve waved as he drove off, then continued his run thinking about everything he wanted to ask this man about Mark.

His hair still damp from the shower, Steve pulled up in front of that large house and walked across the street to the gate, a carrier bag of beer in one hand, his bathing suit in the other. Pushing the buzzer, he heard Jack's voice, then the black wrought iron gate swung back for him to enter. As he approached the front door, Jack was there, smiling at him.

"Hey," Steve said in greeting.

"Hey. You didn't have to bring anything. We're very well stocked." He took the bag and looked in.

"I just thought it would be polite. Just stick it with your own stash." He looked around the light airy rooms and inhaled deeply as if he could catch a trace of Mark's cologne.

"Come on through the house," Jack shouted back to him as he led the way. "I was sitting out back by the pool."

"Cool." Steve followed him in and out of the living area and sliding doors. As Jack stuffed the beer into a cooler, Steve sat down on a lounge chair and admired the shining water and immaculate pool area. "This is great. My place doesn't have a pool. I did consider getting one, but I just didn't know how much I would use it."

"We're in it almost every night." Jack offered one of the chilled beers.

Steve checked the early hour on his watch, then shrugged and reached out for it.

"Did you have breakfast? There are some bagels left."

"Don't go to any trouble, Jack." Steve used a bottle opener and cracked open the beer.

"No trouble. I'll be right back."

After he left, Steve mumbled, "Christ, I clould get used to this."

In a few minutes Jack brought out a tray of sliced bagels, cream cheese and smoked salmon. He set it down in the shade under an umbrella and waved for Steve to dig in. Steve hopped up from his lounge chair and sat down at the table, taking a plate. "Looks great, thanks."

Joining him, Jack began spreading the cream cheese on half a bagel and then asked, "How's it going over at Parsons & Company?"

"All right. Did Mark tell you I got a new account and a promotion?"

"No. He never mentioned it. Congratulations."

"Thanks." Steve bit into the sandwich he had made and chewed it happily.

"He doesn't talk about work much. He's been really preoccupied with this wedding."

After swallowing and taking a sip of beer, Steve replied, "Yeah, about that... Uh, what's the deal with him and Sharon? I mean, do you really think it'll last?"

"Who knows? Does any marriage last?" Jack licked the cream cheese off his finger.

"Well, no, but this one seems to be doomed from the start."

Stopping what he was doing, Jack met Steve's eyes and seemed to grow slightly hostile at the comment.

Shaking off that threatening glance, Steve said, "Come on, Jack. Tell me you don't see it."

"See what...?" Jack asked very suspiciously.

Suddenly Steve felt as if perhaps he shouldn't go in that direction. This handsome blond has been trying to get into Mark's trousers for decades and didn't succeed. How quickly would that friendly demeanor change if he knew he'd had the forbidden fruit?

When Steve didn't answer, Jack said, "He's not gay, Steve, if that's what you're thinking. He's just too sensuous for his own good."

Choking at the truth in that statement, Steve quickly covered his expression of irony and replied, "So...you don't

109

think he could be gay…or bi?"

"No. Look, Steve, I'm gay. If anyone should know if Mark is, it would be me. I've been in love with him since we were in college together. He's not interested."

"You don't think it's you he's not interested in and not other men in general?"

That defensive anger surfaced again suddenly. "No, offense!" Steve added quickly, "Jack you're fantastic looking, and your body…well, it's fucking perfect."

Raising his eyebrows up in surprise, Jack asked, "Are you gay?"

That posed a very interesting question for Steve. Was he? Did one or two sexual encounters with the same sex qualify you? "Uh…"

Resuming his eating, Jack said, "Well, if you are, you're barking up the wrong tree with Mark. Believe me."

"You're sure?" Steve stuffed the rest of his bagel into his mouth.

"Yes. Look, he's been harassed non-stop, especially from his old man, who, thank fuck, is now dead, about being gay. He isn't gay."

"Hmm," Steve nodded, as if thinking about the response. "So you think this marriage with him and Sharon is a good thing?"

"I suppose. In reality I don't want him to be married to her. He'll move out when they tie the knot. She refused to live here if I was here, and I suppose that's reasonable. She's always felt she's in competition with me for some reason, but it's never been what she's thought it was."

"Physical."

"Yes, physical."

"So, you've never kissed Mark, or touched him sexually."

"Well, not never. I do tease him a little, you know."

"But he never reciprocates."

Pausing, looking at Steve with deep interest, Jack asked, "What the hell is all this about? What does it have to do with your working relationship?"

"Absolutely nothing."

"Then why the hell are you so interested in him?"

Again, lost for a reply that wouldn't drop him into a mess, Steve didn't answer.

"You're hot for him." Jack smiled wryly. "Am I right?"

"Uh…"

"You fell for him!" Jack laughed. "Christ, he has the strongest animal magnetism in a man that I have ever seen!"

"Uh…" Steve wiped his lip with the napkin and drank more beer, completely sure if he said another word Jack would hit him.

"Fucking Richfield," Jack shook his head, chuckling about it. "Does he know?"

"Err…" Steve finished the beer and set the bottle down.

"He doesn't?" Suddenly Jack found the situation amusing. "Should I tell him?"

"No. I don't think that's a good idea. He'd be upset I was discussing it with you."

"Why? I think he'd be very flattered. I mean, look at you."

"What?" Steve sat up.

"Well, you're incredible looking."

"Am I?" Steve grinned.

"Oh yes," Jack's tone became seductive.

"Huh…" Steve sat back and digested the compliment.

"You…you want to go to my room and screw?"

Jerking his head to that inviting smile, Steve blinked his eyes in shock. Though the idea was tempting, he thought the relationship he had with Mark was complicated enough. "Wow, Larsen, I am really flattered, honest."

"But?" Jack reached out and touched Steve's arm.

"Uh, but, I've got to go." Steve moved to leave, pushing out the chair to get up.

"You just got here. And you brought your suit so I assumed you'd take a dip."

"Shit," Steve breathed in panic, then said, "I just

remembered something I need to do." When he stood, Jack did as well.

"I didn't mean to make you uncomfortable."

"No...no...not at all, Jack. I've taken it in the right way. No offense whatsoever."

"You sure? You don't need to go. I'll lay off."

Finding his bathing suit and grabbing it, Steve tilted his head to the sliding door. "No, Jack, it's okay. I have to go by my mom's anyway."

Jack escorted him to the front of the house. Before Steve left, Jack closed in on him and leaned on him. "If you change your mind..." he purred.

The goose bumps rising on Steve's arm at so wonderful an invitation, he cleared his throat awkwardly and jumped out of his skin when the front door opened from the outside.

"What the devil is going on here?" Mark choked in anger and shoved his way in.

Steve stumbled back and widened his eyes in surprise.

Calmly, Jack asked, "Where's Sharon?"

"I dropped her off at her mum's. What are you doing here, Steve?"

"I...I..." Steve pointed to Jack then himself.

Jack clarified, "I met him when he was out jogging and asked him back to the house. Unfortunately he's escaping because I made a pass at him."

Holding his breath to see how Mark would respond to that news, Steve waited nervously.

Mark snarled, "I'm glad you're going."

"Right. Sorry. See you at work Monday, Mark?"

Without a word, Mark walked into another room in the house. As if making excuses for him, Jack whispered, "I think this wedding is stressing him out. Don't worry."

"No...I understand. Thanks, Jack."

"No problem."

After Jack closed the door and Steve walked back to his car, he sighed unhappily wondering if this thing with Mark wasn't becoming more of a pipe dream than a reality.

After he had left, Mark poured himself a drink of cognac and stared off into space. He knew if he didn't make a decision a handsome man like Steve wouldn't be available for long. Watching Jack clearing up the tray of food out on the patio, he suddenly envied him and wished he was out in the open about his homosexual feelings, and could make choices freely.

"You okay, Mark?" Jack asked on his way to the kitchen, the tray in his hands.

"Hmm? Yes. Just tired... Uh, Jack..." Mark followed him to the kitchen as he put the food back into the refrigerator.

"Yeah?"

"Do you think I'm doing the right thing? Marrying Sharon?"

Jack turned around and stared at him for a moment, then replied, "Steve asked me the same damn thing. Look, Mark, if you have any doubts, don't do it."

Nodding, sipping his drink, Mark agreed, "Yes, absolutely...don't do it if you have doubts...yes."

After washing up the few dishes, Jack wiped his hands on a towel and then faced him. "What's going on? You were so sure about it."

"I'm not any longer." Mark shivered in fear, knowing he couldn't tell Jack the truth.

"What's happened? I don't get it, Mark. I thought the two of you were pretty well matched."

When Jack moved closer and stroked his hair back from his forehead, Mark instantly got an image of Steve doing the same thing to him and closed his eyes to enjoy the memory.

"Mark?"

Opening them up quickly, Mark backed away from Jack's caress and said, "I just don't know what to do anymore."

113

As Jack walked out of the room, he shouted, "Well, you better decide soon…it's coming up."

Standing alone with his cognac, Mark knew precisely what he should do, he just had to find the courage to do it.

Chapter Twelve

"Are their web-based ads up to date?" Steve asked Roland as they sat together in the conference room, files spread out over the table.

"I think so. We've been mostly dealing with media, both television and print." Roland adjusted his glasses higher on his nose.

"And the list of products is complete, as far as you know?"

"Well, no…they have some new items being revealed this year and I'm waiting for the information on how they want to promote them."

Rubbing his face, Steve was beginning to think this account was completely in need of reorganizing. Obviously, knowing he was retiring soon, Roland had not kept his books and records up to date. "Right…and the name of the contact at Foist that I need to liaise with is Andrew Lloyd?"

"I'll double check that. I don't know if he's still handling it or not."

About to shout out an expletive of complete frustration, Steve bit his lip and wished someone else had been saddled with this mess.

Just then Mark walked past the conference room with a fresh cup of coffee.

"Hang on a moment, Roland…let me just take a break." Roland nodded, adjusting his glasses again and looking through the paperwork as if he were lost.

"Mark...Mark...hang on."

Mark paused, looking back at him, an expression of weariness on his face.

"I need your help."

"You need more than my help. Go find a shrink."

"Mark," Steve spoke softly, then grabbed his elbow as he turned away, almost making Mark spill his coffee. The look of impatience surprised Steve.

"Stop man-handling me."

"I thought you liked it?" Steve whispered close to his ear, "I found my cuffs." Looking for a reaction, Steve smiled when Mark closed his eyes as if he were trying not to get too excited at the idea. "Look," he began again, "Roland has completely fucked up the account paperwork. I can't even figure out who the contact at Foist is, or if their product line is up to date. It's a fricken quagmire. Can I ask Harold if you can help me?"

Mark faced him full on. "Work with you? Sit in an office with you and work with you? Next to you? Physically next to you all day? Do you think that's wise?"

Peering around them first to see who was in hearing range, Steve then smiled wickedly and hissed, "Yesss..."

"Oh, I don't know...you wanted the bloody account, you're the one with the promotion...why should I?"

"Because you love me..." Steve grinned, then added, "And because I need you."

Mr. Parsons appeared around the cloth divider. "A problem, gentlemen?"

Instantly Steve released Mark's arm. "Well, yes, Harold..." Steve said as Mark tried to look innocent of all wrong doing. "Can I speak to you in your office a moment? With Mark?"

Mark cleared his throat awkwardly.

Mr. Parsons nodded and led them to his office. Once they were inside, Steve shut the door. He declined the offer of a chair and waited until the other two men sat down.

Mark sipped his coffee as he listened.

"Harold, Roland has just begun going over the paperwork with me on this account..."

"Yes?"

"...and no offense to him, boss, but it's a mess. Even he can't make heads or tails out of it."

"Really? I assumed it'd been running smoothly. No one has ever complained."

"I don't want there to be any complaints. But his sense of organization is appalling. No offense to him, boss."

Mark chuckled softly.

"I want Mark," Steve said boldly. When Mark choked on his sip of coffee, Steve hid his grin, knowing how he said it would be slightly controversial from Mark's perspective.

Nodding, Mr. Parsons waited for him to continue.

"Look, Harold, let him help me. Just to get it organized."

Mr. Parsons looked at Mark. "I'm not sure that's fair, Steve. After all, you are the one who got the promotion and will get the money for the account."

"Give Mark the promotion as well. Let's split the commission. Look, all that talk about team work and leadership we were given at the retreat, let's put it into practice. I need him as my partner."

Mark shot him another wry glance at his choice of words.

Coughing to clear his throat, Harold asked Mark, "What do you think, Richfield? I know you have a full work load already. Are you willing to give Steve some help?"

After a long pause Mark asked, "This means a promotion and half the commission from the account?"

Steve rolled his eyes, wanting this to be about more than position and money. Whatever happened to true love?

"I can't see how that would be a problem. And I agree with Steve in the matter of team building. He's right. What good was all that money spent on the retreat if we don't get anything out of it but sunburn?" Mr. Parsons said.

"Come on, Mark…help me out," Steve pleaded.

Turning in his chair to him, Mark appeared to be weighing up the pros and cons, something Steve did on a regular basis with every important decision in his life. Finally he said, "All right."

Restraining his urge to pump his fist and jump in the air, Steve just held out his hand and reached for Mark's. When Mark shook it, Steve used his middle finger to tickle his palm seductively. In surprise, Mark drew back and gave him a reprimanding look.

"Fine." Mr. Parsons stood and gestured to the door. "I'll make a memo about it and get it circulated."

Steve opened the office door. "You have time now?" he asked Mark.

"Give me a moment to make a few phone calls."

"Okay." As Mark walked down the corridor to his office, Steve grinned wickedly at that masculine strut. Before he dashed back to a waiting Roland, he caught Charlie watching him curiously. Disregarding his suspicious gaze, Steve headed back to the conference room and began the ordeal of sorting through the mountain of paperwork.

After they had come back from lunch, Mark began sorting each piece of paper from the overstuffed file into stacks of items to be shredded and one for current information. As Steve entered the office, Mark looked up at him, shaking his head. "It's a bloody nightmare."

"I know. It sucks. Why do you think I was begging you to help me out on it?" Steve removed his suit jacket and draped it over a chair, then rolled up his sleeves.

"I have no idea how Roland kept any track of the items and their promotion. It's a wonder to me he got away with it for so long."

"I think most of the work was in place and he just let the machine keep cranking on."

"Absolutely incredible. It'll take hours to get through it."

118

Steve checked his watch. "I know."

As someone stepped in, they both looked up to see the older gentleman coming in, rubbing his glasses in a cloth.

"Uh, Roland," Steve said, "Mark's going to help me out."

"Oh? You need help? I never needed help on the account. I'm surprised."

"Just to get me organized, Roland. No big deal." Steve smiled.

"All right, Steven, if you need it."

Mark looked up at the man as he leaned over his shoulder curiously. "I'm sorting through the old paperwork to shred. It's over five years old, mind." Mark held up a dated page.

"Shredding paperwork?" Roland seemed flustered by the idea.

"Yes," Steve agreed. "It's just clogging up the file. It's old out of date information and it's a good idea to purge it."

"If you think so. I never get rid of any of it. I find you never know when you need to go back to it."

Steve and Mark exchanged glances, then Steve said, "Have a seat, Roland. Show me which radio stations run which ads."

When the man began shuffling through papers again, Steve loosened his collar and tie tiredly, rubbing his head in disbelief.

By six p.m. Mark with sitting at a laptop computer while Steve read off information from paperwork for him to enter on the computer files. Only a few employees were still on hand in the office. Steve noticed Roland looking very weary. "Let us handle it, Roland. Why don't you go home and get some rest?"

"I do need to get home for dinner." He stood up stiffly.

"No problem. I think we can handle it from here. You can help us again in the morning."

119

"All right, Steven. I do need to go."

Steve walked him to the conference room door and patted his back. "Good night."

"Good night, Steven."

As he watched him go, Steve looked over the dividers to see how many people were still lingering. About half a dozen were on telephones or at their computers.

"What a bloody nuisance," Mark sighed.

"I just don't think he was comfortable using a computer." Steve stood behind Mark again as he filled in the information on the screen.

"He has a secretary and he has a PA, there's no excuse."

"Cut him some slack. He's old."

After glimpsing up at him quickly Mark sighed and said, "Right...keep going, we're almost done."

Reaching for a stack of paper, Steve inhaled tiredly, then read the item name and began listing its present marketing strategy. Keeping up, Mark's fingers flew over the keys with tiny clicks.

Someone passed the glass front of the conference room and shouted good-night to them. At the distraction they paused what they were doing and waved at Bret as he passed.

Once Steve had come to the end of one stack of paperwork, he checked his watch again. "You want to call it quits and begin in the morning? There's really no reason to kill ourselves and get this mess all organized now."

Pushing away from the table tiredly, Mark ran his hand through his hair and then stretched his back out. "Yes. I suppose it's been screwed up for this long, what's one more day."

Moving behind his chair, Steve rested his hands on Mark's shoulders and began massaging them gently.

"Ohhh...that's excellent," Mark groaned.

"I know how bad it is sitting and typing on that thing." He noticed a few lights flick off in the main office. "I wonder who's left?"

"Oh. Good point. I don't think it's a good idea for you to be doing that." Mark moved away from his hands.

"You want to catch some dinner and go back to my place?"

Mark read his watch and then rubbed his face again tiredly.

"Please?" Steve whispered, moving closer to him. Unable to resist, he caressed Mark's soft hair, running it through his fingers gently.

Opening his eyes after rubbing them, he noticed someone standing near the conference room door. "Charles?"

Steve dropped his hand quickly and spun around, the picture of guilt.

"You need something?" Mark asked him.

"I hear you two are splitting the Foist account." Charlie leaned against the door, his expression appearing to give away his thoughts more than his words.

"Yeah," Steve replied. "It's a mess. I asked Harold if Mark could help me out."

Nodding as if he understood, Charlie said, "Good thing you two got over your differences in the desert, huh?"

The sarcasm behind the comment made Steve wince.

"Anything else to add, Charles?" Mark sneered.

"No. Nothing at all."

When he left without another word, Steve let out a long exhale and then said, "Shit."

"I warned you about touching me here. I warned you!" Mark rose up and pointed an accusing finger into Steve's face.

"I barely touched you. And besides, he doesn't know anything for sure. He's just fishing around." Steve grabbed his jacket from off the back of the chair. "Come to my place."

"I can't handle anyone here knowing, Steve. Honestly. If I find gay pornography on my desk in the morning, I'll have a nervous breakdown."

121

"You will not. Will you cut out the dramatics?" Steve waited as he closed down the computer program, then shut the light off in the room.

"You don't know the half of it, Steve. The shite I've endured over this issue. I can scream just thinking about it."

Steve followed him to his office where Mark got his things together. "That's why you feel you need to marry this woman, isn't it? Just to put that rumor to rest? What crap."

"That's not the reason. I do resent that comment, Steve." Mark folded his suit jacket over his arm and shut off the light.

They stopped by Steve's office next. He grabbed his briefcase and looked around before he closed the door behind him. "Of course you resent it, because it's the truth. Why the fuck don't you just come out of the closet and get over it?"

"Oh? Have you? Have you told your father and mother you're in love with a man? You having a laugh, Steve?" Mark followed him to the lobby and allowed the cleaning crew in as they left.

"I don't need to tell my mommy and daddy everything about my life." Steve pushed the elevator button.

"Oh, that's the excuse then? Not *my father the bigot/homophobe will end my life*? Give it a rest, will you?" Mark shook his head.

The moment Steve realized they were alone in the elevator, he spun around, grabbed Mark and kissed him passionately. At the surprise, Mark stumbled backwards and fell against the wall of the elevator, grunting in shock.

Once the doors opened to the parking garage, Steve separated from him and stepped out into the open air, smiling. He peered over his shoulder to see Mark trying to recuperate, touching his lips from the sensation.

"Follow me," Steve shouted, like an order.

And nodding his head obediently, Mark obeyed.

Keeping the Mercedes' tail in view, Mark rode the familiar path to Steve's door. He knew he should call someone to tell them he was going to be late, but even the thought of ringing Jack or Sharon was repugnant. He was too tired from all the work of the day and all he wanted was sex. Hot masculine, ex-LAPD-cop sex.

Parking behind him, Mark shut the ignition and stared at him as he climbed out of his car and gathered his things. He could not get enough of looking at him. Instantly he grew excited and anticipated the bout of sex they were going to have. Perhaps Jack didn't turn him on this way. Maybe that was why he couldn't do it with him. What was it about Steve? Even his scent drove him wild.

That masculine tilt of the head summoned him. Mark climbed out of his car and jumped up the steps to his house with a light gate. Once inside, it was as if they were allowed to be themselves. It was private and completely discreet. No Jack to ask him questions, no phone to ring and pry.

Taking the moment to unravel his necktie, Mark stood in the living room and felt as if the stress of his life slipped off his shoulders. After vanishing into another room, Steve emerged dangling silver handcuffs in his fingers.

Instantly, Mark placed his hands behind his back, eager to be the subservient to this powerhouse.

"Wow, you really like this?" Steve laughed.

"Oh, yes. You have no idea…"

"You want a drink first?" Steve set the cuffs down.

"Yes, all right."

"Hungry?" Steve asked as he opened the refrigerator.

"How about a late dinner, after." Mark winked, then took the cold beer from him.

"Perfect." Steve raised the beer bottle to him for a toast. Mark tapped it, and then sipped it down.

After some conversation about work, Steve gestured to his bedroom. Mark hopped off the couch eagerly and began taking off his clothing. "Put on your uniform again."

"Okay." Steve found the shirt and trousers and tossed

them on the bed.

Once Mark was naked, he watched as Steve dressed in the dark clothing. A shiver raced over his skin he was so thrilled at the play acting. "You've just arrested me and I'm in the cell."

"You dirty mother-fucker!" Steve laughed heartily.

Mark blushed in embarrassment. "I feel a bit ashamed. I'm sorry."

Rushing to comfort him, Steve wrapped around him tightly and kissed his cheek. "No need, hot stuff. You should never be embarrassed by it. I'm here to please you, not to judge you. Besides, you have any idea how hard the idea makes me?"

Mark's hand was led to his crotch. "Hard as a brick," Mark whispered, rubbing him.

With his lips under Mark's hair by his ear, Steve whispered, "Tell me what you want me to do."

"Handcuff me, behind my back. Then ride me like a pony..." Mark hissed seductively.

Digging his hands into his hair on both sides of his head, Steve drew that mouth to his first, kissing him so passionately that Mark could feel how much he was loved by the taste. Slowly, Steve parted from his mouth and located the handcuffs, then checked to make sure he did indeed have the key handy. Mark placed his hands behind his back and waited as they were ratcheted on. "Too tight?" Steve asked.

"No. Not in the least."

"Now, listen to me," Steve said, making sure Mark was looking right at him. "You tell me if it's too much and you want to stop. You hear me?"

"Yes. Not to worry."

"Just say something, like, *Hey Copper*. Okay? You say, *Hey Copper*, and I'll stop and cut you loose. Got it?"

"Got it." Mark smiled.

Steve stood back from him and stared at him for a while. Swallowing down his anticipation, Mark stood still waiting. As if it took a moment for Steve to get into his roll, he paused and then finally said, "Right. You know what we do to guys like you?"

Mark shook his head and felt as if his cock was protruding from his body like a flagpole.

"We make 'em pay," Steve hissed wickedly. "And bad boys pay for doing bad things."

"But, officer, I swear I'm innocent." Mark shivered in excitement.

"You may have come in here innocent, but you won't leave that way," he sneered, then laughed. "Come over here."

He grabbed Mark's arm and moved him against the wall of his bedroom. Mark looked up at the ceiling and waited. That luscious pat-down began again, but this time he was stark naked. As those hands ran from his head down his shoulders to his arms, then to his chest and down to his pelvis, Mark couldn't hear anything beyond his own panting and beating heart. Steve brushed by his hard-on quickly, but lingered between Mark's legs, tugging on his balls and pushing into his ass gently. When Mark groaned in delight, Steve grabbed him and escorted him roughly to his bed, then shoved him face up on it. Wincing as the cuffs bit his wrists, Mark turned his head to the side to see him, trying to shake the hair from his eyes. Steve had set out some lubrication, rubbers, and baby oil on the nightstand.

The cuffs felt odd on his wrists, though they weren't tight, they were hard and cold.

Laughing with intentional callousness, Steve poured some oil into his palm and then rubbed them together to make them slick. Then, while Mark's chest was rising and falling rapidly, Steve rubbed the oil all over Mark's skin, coating him so he shined, pinching his nipples until they were tiny erections.

Once Mark was gleaming with it, Steve began removing his uniform shirt. Mark was breathing so quickly he felt he couldn't gain air. When that shirt fell and that wall of muscled chest appeared, Mark crossed his legs to try and stop the incredible urge he had to hump something.

Kicking his trousers aside, Steve dove on Mark and slithered all over his greased body, rubbing his hands over Mark's face, hair, sides, under his arms, then down to his hips and behind his back, lifting Mark off the bed as if he were a rag doll, and rubbing his crotch over his legs and pubic hair. Mark's head was spinning with it. Being helpless, used and fondled by this ex-cop was so sublime he never knew anything physical could be so earth-shattering.

Rolling him over, face down, Steve knelt behind him, putting on a rubber and then spreading the lubrication on himself. Rubbing his rough five o'clock shadow all over Mark's buttocks first, nipping the taut skin there, Steve finally pushed inside that lovely tight opening and gritted his teeth. "Oh, Mark…oh, my fucking god, Mark…"

And feeling that organ pulse inside him, the sound of that pleasure in Steve's voice, was worth everything. "Fuck me, fuck your slave…" Mark crooned back.

His rump high in the air, his hands behind his back, his head against the soft pillows, Mark could feel Steve savoring the moment, pushing deeper inside him Feeling Steve drop down to rest on his back, Steve's hands teasing his cock, rubbing over his chest, his thighs, was making him dizzy. That lovely sensation of being penetrated by someone he absolutely adored, it was so incredible to be receiving that hot masculine man, loving every moment of it, Mark began whimpering in a soft sensual moan. The skin between them began to sweat from the friction and hot contact. Mark closed his eyes as his cock was played with, his balls were tugged gently, and the back of his neck was licked and kissed. Yearning for Steve's orgasm, when it hit and he felt the deep pressure from Steve's hips, felt that throbbing and the sense of being filled with lava, Mark shivered in pleasure and knew this man was everything he

126

had ever wanted in a lover.

Once Steve pulled out and removed the condom, Mark felt the cuffs opening, freeing his hands. Lovingly, Steve rubbed the marks they had made on them, then tossed them on the floor. Allowing Mark to lie on his back, Steve crawled over the bed to him and asked, "What do you want me to do? It's your turn."

"I want your hands, then your mouth, then your ass," Mark panted, his hair sticking to his sweaty forehead and neck.

"You got it…" Steve grinned. Mark spread his legs and reached for both of Steve's hands, placing them on his cock.

Sitting up next to him, Steve slowly smoothed up and down that incredible length. "What a cock you have, Richfield…what an amazing cock…"

Watching him, pacing himself so he didn't come too fast, Mark kept moving his gaze from Steve's face and body, to those rough masculine hands. "Suck it."

Immediately complying, Steve lowered down, holding the base, and shut his eyes in pure delight. Unable to prevent it, Mark closed his eyes and groaned, his hips moving in time with that hot mouth. Steve's tongue teasing the tip, swirling around it and lapping at it as if it were something to devour, Mark had to hold back with everything he had to not come in his mouth. Steve sat back and smiled at him. "Time to fuck the cop?"

Mark grinned demonically. Steve scrambled to his knees and waited. Finding the lubrication and rubbers within reach, Mark slid one on, coated himself efficiently, and then knelt behind this lovely male. Once he was on target, he pushed in with a hiss of air through his teeth and savored the penetration. Feeling Steve blindly reaching behind him, Mark gave him one of his hands and immediately was led back to Steve's cock. Smiling knowingly, Mark masturbated him as he pumped, leaning over his smooth back, and licking the salty sweat from it. His hips moving deeper and faster, Mark spun into a devastating climax as if he had never experienced one before. The intensity distracting Mark temporarily, Steve gripped Mark's hand and pumped with him furiously, coming instantly and grunting in pleasure at his second orgasm of the night.

Completely sated, Mark dropped down on Steve's back and tried to catch his breath, just managing to get rid of the spent rubber. Before they both realized it, they had fallen into a deep slumber.

Chapter Thirteen

Very gently, Steve rolled over, smiling, cuddling the warm body next to him. Feeling some movement from it, he crooned, "Oh, my baby…you are so fucking hot."

"Hmmm?"

"Let's fuck again…" Steve nestled into Mark's neck, licking his skin, then moved his hands to Mark's pelvis and bumped into a very hard cock.

"What time is it?" Mark asked groggily.

"Time?" Suddenly Steve felt disoriented. He sat up and looked for his alarm clock. The digital numbers read 9:14 a.m. It took him some time to think with any clarity.

When Mark didn't receive an answer, he sat up and looked for himself. "Please don't tell me that says a quarter past nine."

As if struggling for an answer, Steve sat up and looked around the room. On the floor was his old police uniform and a pair of silver handcuffs, spent condoms near them, and Mark's suit trousers and cotton shirt. "Shit."

Mark leapt out of bed and spun around as if he didn't know what to do first. "We're both late? After working late together! Oh, this won't look good! Steve, this won't look good!"

"Calm down. Let me call work and I'll just tell them something. Go take a shower."

After Mark left, Steve sat up on the edge of the bed and

concentrated. He picked up the phone and dialed. "Ray? Yes, it's Steve…look, can you tell Harold that Mark and I got out of the office very late last night and we decided to come in just a little later this morning? Good. Ah…about an hour or so? Yes. Thanks, Ray. Bye." He hung up and rubbed his rough jaw, then stood and scratched his balls as he tried to think.

Lathering up, trying not to think of the implications of not coming home last night, Mark didn't know what would be worse: dealing with the odd stares at work, or Jack and Sharon's barrage of questions once they exchanged notes. When the bathroom door opened he jumped, startled, then found Steve's tired unshaven face. "Are we fucked?"

Steve pulled back the shower door and sighed, "Naa, I just told Ray to tell Harold that we decided to come in late since we were there late. No biggie."

"Oh. All right." Mark rinsed the soap from his hair. "I dread stopping home for a change of clothing. Jack will be at my throat."

"So?" Steve shrugged, "Wear the same thing. No one will notice. You want a pair of my briefs?"

Mark closed the taps and stood dripping. "I'm really making a cock-up of my life, aren't I?"

Before Steve handed him a towel, he leaned down and kissed his cock, then smiled and gave it to him. "No. You're finally doing something you want to do."

Mark rubbed the towel through his hair and stepped out of the shower so Steve could get in. "I wish I could believe that. I'm very anxious at the moment."

Climbing into the shower, Steve turned on the water and started washing. "I know. You really have complicated your life, Mark. You should just come clean to everyone. Tell Sharon, tell Jack…just get it over with."

"That's simple for you to say!" Mark shook his head at the absurdity. "Just tell your father you're gay. All right?

When you do that then you come back to me and tell me what to do."

"It's not the same, Mark."

"Oh?" Mark noticed Steve's brush and started pulling it through his long hair in the mirror.

"No!" Steve shouted over the water noise. "I'm not marrying my father and I don't live with him either. What I do with you makes no difference to his daily life and routine. You see the difference now?"

He did. Frowning at himself in the mirror, Mark wished other people's feelings were not at stake. That was the problem. The selfishness of the act.

Finished washing, Steve shut the water off and stood dripping, staring at Mark. "I want you here. Every day. Can I make it any clearer than that?"

Slowly turning around, Mark stared at that wonderful wet male body, one right off the pages of a sex magazine. "I wish it were that easy."

"It is. Just do it, as they say." Steve smiled, then grabbed a towel to wipe off his wet face.

Staring at that charming grin, Mark knew what he wanted to do, and dreaded doing what he was obligated to do.

They pulled into their side by side parking spaces and then walked to the elevator together. It was nearing 10:30 and Steve was resigned to return any sly comment with anger and aggression.

"He's infuriated with me," Mark sighed as he flipped his mobile phone shut and allowed the elevator door to close behind him.

"Who?"

"Jack. I just returned his call. He had left several messages on my answer service."

"And Sharon as well, I take it." Steve sighed, shaking his head.

"Yes. Her as well."

"Fuck them. You aren't their slave...you're mine," Steve whispered.

"Cheeky monkey," Mark laughed.

"Growl!"

"Calm down, love. We're at our floor." Mark nodded to the numbered light.

The door opened and even though they were coming in together and Mark was in yesterday's suit, and they had both neglected to shave in the rush, they pretended they hadn't just screwed all night and woke up in the same bed.

"Hello, Mary." Steve smiled at her and set his briefcase down on his desk.

"There you are, Steve. Roland is in the conference room sorting through more files. I didn't know when to tell him you would be in. Raymond told me you had called and you would be late."

"Yes." Steve took the coffee cup from her. "Thanks, you're a doll."

"I like the unshaven look. It's very masculine!" she laughed at him in a tease.

He rubbed it and sighed, "No time. Oh well."

"Anything else you need right now?"

"Any calls I have to return?" He sipped the hot brew.

"I've put them off for a day. I know how much time you need on the Foist account."

"You're fantastic. Thanks, Mary."

She blushed at his wink and went back to her desk.

A cup of coffee in his hand, Mark made his way down the hall to the conference room to resume where they had left off the night before. "Good morning, Charles," he smiled as he met him in the hall.

Charlie shook his head at him in disbelief.

"Something on your mind?" Mark asked.

"You're unshaven as well? You both look like you just

climbed out of the sack. Why don't you just admit the two of you had sex in the desert that night?"

Mark choked on his coffee and tried not to spill it.

"Live in denial, Mark, I don't give a shit. You know, no one cares if you guys are gay lovers. I think it's worse when people like you lie about it. And I'm not the only one who feels that way."

When he continued down the hall, Mark felt sick to his stomach. "Great…just great. Oh, this is going to explode like a bleedin' volcano."

Slightly shaken up from the encounter, Mark met Steve coming into the conference room. "We are so screwed," Mark whispered to him.

"Why?" Steve asked quietly.

"Everyone bloody knows!"

"Shut up, they do not. Now just get in there and get Roland to help us." Waiting as he passed him by and sat down at the desk with his laptop, Steve took a paranoid glance around the office and wondered if it really made a difference to the people around him.

Taking a break, Steve headed to the lunch room to pour two fresh cups of coffee to bring back to the conference room. Just as he came through the door the conversation stopped and Bret and Kevin stared at him strangely.

"Something on your mind, guys?" Steve tried not to snarl at them, but the office gossip was getting to him.

"Huh?" Bret shook his head innocently.

Not intimidated by him, Kevin decided to air his suspicions. While Steve was at the coffee pot, Kevin said softly, "You know there're rumors circulating about you guys."

"Why, because we worked together late one night?" Steve stirred milk into his coffee and milk and sugar into Mark's.

"No, not just that." Kevin glanced over at Bret who

seemed very intimidated by Steve and wouldn't add to the conversation.

"Do you know he's engaged to be married next month?" Steve held a mug in each hand, the steam swirling over them like tiny spirits.

"So? He's not married yet."

Kevin peered down at the cups of coffee. "One for you, one for Mark?"

"Yeah, so what? I didn't want to bother Mary for them. She's got enough to do. Can you get the door? Or is that too much to ask?"

Bret rushed to open it for him.

Standing still, Kevin replied, "We're not stupid, Steve. No one in this place is. So why don't you guys just be honest with everyone, and yourselves?"

Pausing before he made it to the hall, Steve turned back avoiding Bret's look of horror and said to Kevin, "Mind your own fucking business. I don't pry into your life, stay the hell out of mine."

"But it is business, Steve. And we're supposed to trust you two."

"Just shut the fuck up and get back to your work." Steve carried the hot coffees down the hall, a cloud of resentment growing around him. If it were up to him, he would tell them. In reality, having sex with someone like Mark wasn't a cause for embarrassment in his book.

He set one steaming mug near Mark, by his laptop.

"Thanks," Mark said, then sipped it quickly.

"You sure I can't get you one, Roland?" Steve sat down next to him.

"No, no, I'm fine, Steven." He pushed his glasses higher on his nose.

Taking a moment to sip his coffee and wait as Mark entered more data on the computer, Steve shuffled through some paperwork and then whispered. "I just had a little run-in with Kevin in the lunch room."

"Oh?" Mark barely looked up from the screen.

"Kevin Wagner?" Roland asked, "A run-in? He's such a nice lad. What kind of run- in?"

Staring straight at Mark, Steve replied, "He thinks there's something going on between me and Richfield."

Mark started coughing in a choking fit and then shook his head at Steve as if to say, *we're not alone!*

It took Roland some time, then he responded, "I don't think it's anyone's business what you two boys do on your own time."

"That's what I thought." Steve sipped his coffee calmly.

"Uh hum?" Mark rolled his eyes in annoyance.

"It's not that, Roland, they just feel we're not being honest with them. You know. Like we're lying, hiding things."

"Steve!" Mark shook his head in disbelief.

"Oh, I see." Roland pushed his glasses against his face again as they slid down his nose. "Well, that is a problem. After all we're a very tightly knit group here. I can understand."

"I felt kinda bad." Steve finished his cup and set it aside, then adjusted a paperwork stack to lie neatly.

"I wouldn't worry about telling the staff the truth," Roland whispered, "No one will judge either of you. It's a very liberal company, boys. Just be yourselves."

"I don't believe this conversation," Mark replied nervously. "I'm going to be married in a few weeks…hello?"

As if the reminder had surprised Roland, he answered very bluntly, "Well, Mark, if I were you I'd put some good hard thought into that. After all, marriage is a lifetime commitment."

"Yes, Mark," Steve smiled impishly, "put some good hard thought into that decision."

"Oh, shut up…give me the next file, will you?"

Steve smiled adoringly at him, then handed him the paperwork.

By five p.m. they were getting ready to leave. Mark was sliding on his jacket tiredly and shutting off the light in his office. When he spun around, Steve was there waiting for him.

"Come home with me."

"I can't, love. I'm already in hot water for last night."

"Then what difference will another night make?"

"I have to get fresh clothing and I do have to explain why I was gone all night. I know it's easy for you to say, 'just do it' but in reality, it means hurting people who are dear to me."

Steve looked around first, then touched Mark's arm lightly. "I know."

"Weddings are so big…so important…that even just the planning is like building a sky-scraper, and once it's almost built, it's a devil to tear down."

"Yes, but once you say 'I do', it's even worse."

His heart aching in his chest, Mark lowered his eyes. "Let me go home, love. Let me try and think this through."

After making sure the halls were vacant, Steve kissed him quickly and whispered, "Just don't forget about me."

"No. No, that won't happen. I can assure you." Mark tried to smile, then followed him out to the parking garage.

Pausing in the car as the wrought iron gate opened, Mark stared at his home and the maroon Jaguar in the drive. Just as he moved his TVR next to it, he noticed Sharon's Land Rover and cringed. Shutting the ignition, Mark sat a moment to try and make a decision. Rubbing his jaw stubble tiredly, he knew no matter which way he went it would be impossible.

As he opened the front door he expected them to be standing there, arms crossed, to confront him. He was surprised no one was there. Setting down his briefcase and then his jacket, Mark moved through the house and then heard the sound of voices and water splashing in the pool. Sliding back the glass doors, the noise became clearer and he could see Jack swimming laps while Sharon sat on the edge kicking her feet in the water.

"Look what the cat finally dragged in," she shouted to Jack sarcastically.

Hearing her shout, he stopped swimming and stood in the pool, looking back at Mark.

"Oi, you all right?" Mark yelled in greeting, knowing he was in the doghouse.

She rolled her eyes in irritation and didn't reply. Immediately Jack climbed out and approached him. "Where the fuck were you? All night? You disappear all night and don't even call either of us? What the hell's going on?"

"Uh...well, I was working late—"

"Wait." Jack held up his hand. "Steve Miller. Right?"

Hearing that name, Sharon climbed to her feet and stormed over. "No!"

Staring from one furious set of blue eyes to the other, Mark knew no amount of lying would convince them. He felt sick.

"I knew it!" Sharon pointed at him. "I could tell by the way you guys were acting! So, you are gay!"

"I don't believe this!" Jack roared.

"No...wait...let me explain..."

"There's nothing to explain, Mark!" Sharon sneered, "You're unshaven and no doubt in yesterday's clothing. Am I right, Jack?"

Jack took a look at the suit Mark was wearing. "What's going on, Mark?"

"Wait...please..." Mark felt a cold sweat break out on his forehead. "Just give me a minute."

"You better tell me if you plan to go through with this wedding," Sharon warned. "Daddy has already spent a fortune on it, and if you aren't marrying me, tell me now!"

"Oh, god..." Mark looked for a chair to sit down on, feeling weak suddenly.

Once he'd dropped down in one, Jack stood over him with his arms crossed in anger. "You want to explain? Go ahead. We can't wait to hear it."

Seeing them hovering over him furiously, Mark rubbed his forehead and sighed. "I didn't intend on it to happen. You must believe me."

Both Jack and Sharon threw up their hands in disgust.

"Wait...hear me out," Mark begged. "Sit...please. Let me get this off me chest."

Reluctantly they sat down, pulling the chairs closer to him.

After they had stopped fidgeting and gave him their undivided attention, Mark whispered hoarsely, "It was that bloody retreat...remember? That team building bullocks?" Jack nodded, Sharon didn't. "Well, they set us up, you see. Parsons wanted to force us into a situation where we would either kill each other or not. He knew how much we hated each other from the moment we met. I told you, we both wanted the same position and large account."

"You don't tell me squat." Sharon rolled her eyes.

"He did tell me." Jack nodded to her.

"Figures," she snorted in reply.

Waiting until they quieted down, Mark continued, "They deliberately made us get lost in the desert. Oh, they had it all planned, the sneaky gits...broken compass, screwed up map, the works. Well, Kevin and Charles are in on it, right. So, they quickly vanished in some sort of feigned panic, making a dash to escape us. By nightfall we were completely lost and freezing our arses off."

"Do I really want to hear this?" Jack rubbed his face in agony.

"You?" Sharon choked at the absurdity.

"Please," Mark implored, "Let me get through it." Once they both nodded, he said, "Make no mistake, I wanted to kill him. I did. Honest. What an arrogant ex-cop, I thought, interested in only himself. Believe me. But, as the temperature dropped, I thought I would die of frostbite. I was shivering, me teeth were chattering."

"So you decided to rub two dicks together to get warm?" Jack sneered sarcastically.

Seeing the pain in his eyes, Mark sank deeper into his guilt. "Yes. Oh, Jack, I am so sorry."

"You're sorry about Jack?" Sharon choked in disbelief.

"No. Both of you." Mark reached out his hands but they weren't received.

"All right," Jack nodded, as if he were being logical about it. "So, you did it that night to keep warm. Okay. So, that was a one off?"

Biting his lip, glancing at Sharon's look of complete devastation, Mark couldn't do it. "Yes. A one off."

"But, where were you last night?" she asked.

"I did go back to his place, but just to sleep."

"Yeah, right!" Sharon shook her head at the absurdity.

"Come on, Mark..." Jack stood up defiantly.

As if she were weighing it out, Sharon rose up and faced Mark as he slouched in the deck chair. "So? You got your yaya's out, and now you're ready for marriage?"

Tears beginning to run down his face, Mark wanted to please her despite his real feelings. He knew how much this wedding meant to her. "Yes..."

She sat on his lap and stared at his face closely. "You're sure?"

More salty warm tears rushed to his cheeks. "Yes..."

When she embraced him, Mark looked over her shoulder to see Jack's jealousy and doubt. The betrayal appeared to have been more severe with him than it was with her. And that was just one of the ironies of his life.

Chapter Fourteen

On Saturday morning when the phone rang, Steve rushed to get it. "Hello?"

"Steven, it's your mother."

Deflated, he sat down on his bed and breathed, "Hi…"

"You all right? You sound tired."

"Yes…I'm fine. What's up?"

"Your father was going to invite Laura and her family over this afternoon for a barbeque. Are you free?"

Seeing as Mark wasn't answering his calls and refused to commit to anything when they last were together in the office on Friday, Steve replied, "What time?"

Early afternoon, Steve parked in front of that house with the wrought iron gate and noticed there were no vehicles parked in the drive. "More wedding plans, Richfield?" he mumbled sadly. "Why am I doing this to myself? Why?"

Placing the car in drive, he continued down the wide avenue and decided to stop at Laura's house before they all gathered at his parents' place for dinner.

Glancing back at his car once, he then stuffed his keys into his shorts' pocket and walked up the paved path to her front door. Even before he rang the bell he could hear his niece crying on the other side. Smiling sadly to himself, he rang the bell and waited patiently.

A hurried Barry answered. "Oh! Hi, Steve. Come in. Laura, Steve is here!"

She appeared with a weepy Chloe in her arms and asked, "Were we expecting you?"

"No. Sorry. I just decided to stop by before we headed to Mom's."

"Come in...you want a beer?" she asked, then handed her daughter to Barry.

"Yeah, why not." Steve patted the toddler's head, then followed his sister to the kitchen. "I didn't mean to screw up your schedule."

"No, you're not. She's just woke from a nap and gets a little grouchy. You okay? Things going okay at work?"

Steve took the beer and glimpsed back at Barry who set Chloe down on the floor gently. The little one took one step, sat down and then cried again. "Oh, dear..." Steve smiled at his sister. "Looks like we're not ready for the rest of the day yet."

"She'll settle down. Barry, why don't you put her in her highchair? I'll give her some food. That shuts her up."

Barry picked up the imp who was in the throes of a tantrum and tried to get her in the chair and strapped in.

"Better you guys, than me!" Steve shook his head.

"Don't want kids?" Barry asked, appearing slightly worse for wear.

"Naaa...not me...anyway..." Steve watched as his sister handed the child some food, which instantly shut her up.

"Yes...?" Laura sat down next to her daughter and then gave Steve her attention. "So, what's happening with this English guy you were competing with for that account?"

"I had sex with him."

At the bluntness of the comment, Barry choked in surprised.

Laura laughed and then said, "You are so full of shit."

"Well," Steve clarified, "we screwed each other. I didn't just screw him...anyway, I'm madly in love with the guy."

"Are you serious? You are in love with a man now? Is

that your latest fetish?"

"Fetish?" Steve had to smile.

"Yes. First a black woman, now a man? What's next? A cow?"

"Ouch!" Steve cracked up and then peeked at Barry who appeared fascinated, but not in a good way. "No. I draw the line at bovines. Look, just because I have exotic tastes doesn't mean you should judge me. There was certainly nothing wrong with Sonja. She was absolutely fantastic."

"Yes. I won't disagree with that. I always wondered what she saw in you."

"Laura...do you enjoy picking on me?" Steve was beginning to lose his humor.

"No. Sorry. Okay, so this guy...what's he like?"

"Christ, Laura, he is absolutely fantastic as well. As gorgeous as Sonja."

"Get out," she laughed, shaking her head.

"I'm not kidding. He's tall, slim, fit, and has long brown hair and bright green eyes. Oh, and you'd love his accent. He's a Brit."

"Oh? Bad teeth, then?" she grinned.

"Naaa, a shining movie star smile. And the penis on him...holy crap."

"Uh hum?" Barry nodded to Chloe, who was covered in jam and bread, eating happily.

"She can't understand, Barry." Laura gave her brother back her attention. "So? When can we meet Mr. Wonderful?"

"I don't know. He's got some stupid fiancé and is supposed to get married next month." When Steve finished his beer he noticed both his sister and brother-in-law gaping at him strangely. "What?" he asked.

"Engaged?" Laura tilted her head at him.

"Yeah... a technicality."

"Ya think?" she laughed, then shook her head at her husband.

"Does she know?" Barry asked.

"She knows we work together. And she does suspect something. But I have no idea if she has been told we've actually done it."

"And she still wants him?" Barry choked.

Shrugging, Steve spun the beer bottle in his hand and then stared at his sister. "I'm crazy about him, Laura. Even more than I was about Sonja."

"How can that be possible? You were head over heels for her."

"Because...he's everything I have ever wanted in a partner."

Rubbing her head as if it ached, Laura sighed, "Why do you do this to yourself? What about Mom and Dad? Can you imagine Dad knowing you're gay?"

"I know. I'd have to move." Steve stood and set the bottle on the counter.

"Don't tell him," Barry said.

Laura found some baby wipes and cleaned up Chloe's hands and face. "You can't mention it to them, Steve. Just say you're celibate when they ask about who you are dating."

"It won't go anywhere anyway," Barry added. "The guy's going to be married soon. I assume that means he'll stop playing around."

Sinking at the comment, Steve leaned back on the counter and watched his sister tend her child. Would that mean the end? The end of something that hasn't even begun yet?

When she had cleaned up Chloe, Laura looked back at Steve. "He's right, you know. Maybe it's time to date around again."

"I don't want to date around. I already know there's no one out there to compete with him."

"Yes, but now that you have men as an option, how do you know that for certain?"

"Believe me, I know."

"I need to get her ready for Mom and Dad's." Laura

143

checked her watch.

Steve nodded. "You want me to drive us all there?"

"Naaa, the car seat is too much a pain in the butt to get in and out. We'll follow you." She took Chloe out of the chair and carried her out of the room. "Be back!"

Steve nodded, then looked at Barry, who was daydreaming. "You think I'm nuts, don't you?"

Barry met his eye. "No. Not nuts. I suppose you can't help who you like. It's just that the decisions you're making are very complicated. I'd always opt for the easy route. Life's hard enough."

"I wish it was the easy route. Christ, Barry, you think I don't know what we're up against?"

"You mean what you're up against. He's going to be a husband next month."

Withstanding the words as if they were blows from a fist, Steve stood there like a statue as the other two got their daughter ready and loaded the car.

"Mark?...Mark?"

"Hmmm?" he answered.

"Are you asleep? Hello? It's as if you're a million miles away." Sharon nudged him. "Come on, help me decide on what song the band will play for our first dance."

"Anything is fine, love." Mark hardly glanced at the pages of music to select from.

"But, we don't really have 'our song'."

"No. No, we don't have our song," he echoed softly, his eyes unfocused.

"Do you have any favorites?"

"What? Favorites?"

"Maaark!" she shouted in exasperation. "If you don't want to do this, tell me now!"

Finding her eyes instantly, he couldn't help but feel complete panic at either telling her the truth or going through with it. A rock and a hard place, that's where he had found himself. "A song…a song…uh, how about *Love me do* by the Beatles."

"You are really silly." She smiled at him, then continued to flip through the music sheets.

To himself he muttered, "Silly…yes, that's me…silly."

"How about something from Streisand? Her songs are always romantic."

"What? No, that's too cliché and sappy. No."

She stared at him a moment, then continued to flip the sheets as if one of the pages would jump out at her.

His hands becoming cold and clammy, Mark knew the time was growing tight on this decision. If he wasn't going to say 'I do', he had better do something. "Sharon?"

"Yeah?" She continued to search for the mystery song.

"Uh…uh…" When she finally turned to look at him, the expression on her face appearing a little weary from all the nagging decisions to make, he said, "How about *Only fools fall in love*?"

"Prefect." She grinned and pecked his lips.

Trying to smile as she stood to tell the man she had made a choice, Mark checked his watch and then ran his fingers through his hair tiredly, wondering what Steve was doing right at that moment.

"Another beer, Steve?"

"Okay, thanks, Dad." Steve reached for the bottle and then twisted open the top. Chloe was in her grandmother's arms, pointing to everything in the backyard as grandma patiently told her what each item was. His belly full of food, Steve felt groggy and imagined an afternoon nap.

Barry and Laura were reclining on two lounge chairs, staring at grandmother and granddaughter simply because they were the only thing to watch at the moment.

"When are you going to meet a nice woman, Steve?" Dick asked after getting another beer for himself.

The question inevitable and predictable each and every

visit, Steve shrugged and didn't answer.

Laura glanced at Barry, then Steve before she answered, "He's better off on his own, Dad. Stop asking him."

"He's in his mid-thirties, Laura, and he's not getting any younger." Dick scratched at his arm distractedly. "Maybe your mother knows a nice girl from church."

Rolling his eyes at the repetitiveness of the conversation, Steve ignored him. He knew better than to argue. "You planning on going fishing again, Dad?"

"I don't know. Why? You interested?"

"No. Just making conversation."

In his usual brusque way, Dick asked, "What are your hobbies, Steve? Besides running? What the hell do you do all day?"

Smiling to himself, Steve imagined replying with something very naughty, but decided it would get him into trouble. Laura met his eyes, a sly grin on her face and he knew she knew what he was thinking. "I do nothing all day, Dad. I'm a lazy SOB."

"You got that right," Dick mumbled. "Susan, wasn't there some cake in the house?"

She brought Chloe back to the group and stood bouncing her in her arms. "Yes, you want me to get it now?"

"I'll get it, Mom," Laura offered, then stood up off the chair.

"On the counter, sweetheart, in a white bakery box."

"I'll help her." Steve set his beer down and followed her into the kitchen.

"Get the plates," Laura said, as she cut the string that was around the box and opened it up. "Oooh, yum! Cheesecake!"

Steve removed five plates from the cupboard and set them down. "I need to make a call."

"Oh?" Laura smiled knowingly at him as she cut up neat wedges of cake.

"Yeah. Keep on the look out for me." He nodded to the patio and then picked up his parents' phone. After taking the number from out of his wallet, he dialed Mark's mobile phone number and waited. Finally Mark answered. "Hello?"

"Hey, baby...you busy?" Steve kept his eyes on his father through the glass doors.

"I can't really talk at the moment. Where are you? I don't recognize the number on my display."

"My folk's place."

"Are you going home soon?"

"I can, why? You available?"

"Shit. She's coming. Let me go."

"Ring me later?"

"Yes. Bye, love."

Steve hung up and then stood a moment, enjoying the echo of Mark's voice in his ear, then he blinked his eyes and found Laura staring at him.

"You've got it bad."

"I know. I'm fucking hard as a rock."

"Ew! Shut up!" She shivered comically. "I'd ask you to help me with the cake plates, but you just grossed me out."

Smiling at her, shaking his head, he carried the rest of the plates out to the patio, and began making excuses in his head to go home.

Pacing, looking at the clock as the afternoon ticked by and vanished, Steve picked up the phone to call him, then set it back down. "Fuck this..." he grumbled, then changed into his running gear and warmed up, stretching his muscles. He had to do something to unwind. Waiting for Mark to call was driving him insane. Tying his house key to his shoe, he locked up the front door and then set out for a long mind-numbing run.

Coated in perspiration and gasping for air, Steve sprinted the last few yards to his house, then stopped and bent over, trying to catch his breath. He checked the time, it was nearing seven p.m. Unlacing his shoe, he used his key to get inside the air-conditioned home and then moved directly to his answering machine. No light was flashing. Infuriated by the neglect, he stormed to the kitchen for a bottle of water and fumed.

Chapter Fifteen

Monday morning Steve felt as if he were going through the rote motions of getting ready and driving to work. The TVR was already in its space gleaming in the hot early sunshine. His jaw set, his temper anything but mild, he rode the elevator and headed straight to his office to get his work done. Mary greeted him politely, handed him his coffee and then waited for instructions. "Close the door for me, Mary."

Seeing his foul mood, Mary nodded tacitly and left, closing the door behind her.

Steve immediately immersed himself in his work and set up several appointments to get him out of the building. His keys in one hand, his briefcase in the other, he walked out of his office and heard Mark calling his name. About to continue on his way to the elevator and not stop, Steve inhaled deeply first, then paused, glaring at him from over his shoulder as he tried to catch him, rushing down the corridor.

"Love, sorry, can we talk?"

"I'm on my way to an appointment."

"I'm sorry…let me explain."

"Later. I have to go." Steve twisted away from him and continued to the lobby.

Behind him, a forlorn Mark stared silently.

Making certain he was busy all day, Steve had four more contracts in his briefcase for some minor clients, but they were contracted for three years each. By four thirty p.m. he was back at Parsons & Company and had intentions of dropping off the paperwork and leaving again to go home.

Mark was waiting for him in his office, sitting in Steve's chair behind his desk. When Steve found him there he stopped short at his door and then asked, "You sitting on your ass there all day?"

"No. Just the last half hour."

"I'm leaving. Just stopped here to drop off my paperwork."

"Steve...wait."

Pausing, feeling very angry and impatient, Steve didn't meet his eye.

"Uh...I've made an appointment for the two of us to meet with RJ Foist to go over everything we've updated, etcetera."

"Great." Steve checked his watch and then took a step closer to the hall.

"It's tomorrow. Nine a.m. All right?"

"Yeah, fine, whatever." Steve started to leave.

"Steve, wait! Please."

Seeing several co-workers in the area, and knowing just the idea of Mark having been sitting in his chair for the last half hour was enough to raise eyebrows, Steve sighed in frustration and said, "Look, I got the hint. You're going to be married in two weeks. Okay? I get it."

"Oh, god...wait...Steve." Mark rushed around the desk to prevent him from leaving.

Just as Mark grabbed his arm, Steve noticed Charlie glance over the divider and observe their contact.

"Forget it, Mark." Steve jerked his arm away from him and left, not looking back.

Mark felt sick to his stomach watching that broad back

150

walk away from him. Suddenly noticing Charlie's suspicious stare, Mark returned it with a nasty look of his own and then gathered his things to leave the office.

When he stepped out to the parking garage and the Mercedes was gone, he sat in his car and rubbed his face tiredly.

Steve threw his things down as he walked through his front door. The mixture of anger and hurt was so intense he felt like either punching his fist into a wall or bursting out in painful sobs. Doing neither, he removed his suit jacket and tie, and headed to his refrigerator for some tonic to soothe him. Beer.

Kicking off his shoes, opening the buttons of his shirt, he dropped down on the couch in the den and drank down the cold ale bitterly. "Give up. He's not going to cancel that wedding. Give up." Hearing those words of defeat come out of his mouth was worse than thinking them. Closing his eyes, the agony finally hitting him, he did begin to cry. And as the tears filled his eyes, that soft sobbing increased into that wailing he dreaded so much.

Tuesday morning he set his briefcase on his desk and found a notice for Roland's retirement party. Gazing at the computer generated graphics, he noted the date on his calendar and then tossed the paper in the trash.

A light rap alerted him. He raised his clean shaven jaw to the door.

"You ready?"

Not answering, Steve went to a cabinet and pulled out the large file.

Feeling the ice cold air, Mark kept his conversation a business one. "I've got all the updated work printed out. You can leave those."

Tossing the paperwork back into the file roughly, Steve

slammed the drawer closed and then picked up his briefcase.

"...uh, I've got the new contract renewals as well."

Slamming down his briefcase in fury, Steve shouted, "Then why do you need me to go? You've already got everything you need. Go without me."

"Without you? No. This is your account. Our account. No. I insist you be there with me."

"Oh, screw you, Richfield. Just go and take it. I don't want anything to do with it or you." Steve imagined quitting. No notice, no good-byes, just walking out the door and never coming back.

Peering behind him first, Mark moved closer to Steve's desk and whispered, "It's your account. If anyone should walk away from it, it should be me. I'll go let Mr. Parsons know."

Steve panicked and went after him. "Wait! Are you kidding? He'd fire me because I can't work with you. Don't even try that shit!"

Staring into Steve's hardened gaze, Mark replied, "I'm not trying anything. I just don't want us to fight like this."

"Just get going." Steve shoved him into the hall. As they walked to the elevator, Steve asked, "You sure you have everything?"

"Yes."

They rode the whole way down in silence. Mark chirped the alarm on his sports car and Steve, an avid admirer of sleek automobiles, was having a hard time not crooning and gushing over the tactile rush the interior gave him. Hiding his pleasure at sitting in the bucket seat, which was like a palm of a giant hand cuddling his derriere, Steve discreetly ran his hand over the door and dash, enjoying fondling this super-mobile.

When Mark whispered, "You touch my car the same way you touch me," Steve knew he'd been caught admiring the machine. He didn't reply.

Avoiding Mark's obvious sexual innuendos during the

ride to RJ Foist's high-rise offices, Steve stared out of the window of the car wondering why Mark enjoyed toying with him so much, when the sound of wedding bells must surely be ringing in his head.

After a weekend of no contact from him, Steve decided the only way to deal with his feelings for Mark was on a purely business level. He loved his job and didn't want to be chased out by a bad relationship. He wouldn't be the first to love and break up there, he won't be the last.

They introduced themselves to the receptionist, and Steve allowed Mark to do the talking since it was he who had made the appointment and now held all the paperwork.

In a minute a woman came to meet them and nodded for them to follow. Steve trailed behind Mark trying not to stare at the way his suit jacket fit around his waist and flared at his bottom, but inevitably he was mesmerized by it.

"Mr. Foist will join you in a moment. Would either of you care for a cup of coffee?"

Steve shook his head no and Mark did the same as he set his briefcase and laptop down on the conference table.

"You all right?" Mark asked as he booted up the computer.

Steve stood near him, watching the screen and the icons appear. He nodded but didn't say anything.

Ten minutes later an imposing older gray-haired gentleman and his entourage of three entered the room extending hands to greet them and making the introductions.

Opening the button of his suit jacket, Steve sat next to Mark who was already explaining the new marketing strategies for the expensive items they were going to advertise. As if he were only a spectator in this meeting, Steve leaned back to observe as this English stud charmed his way into the bank accounts of this mega company. His green eyes twinkled with his smile, his wink was taken as kindness and devotion, not lasciviousness, his long hair, which seemed slightly too radical at times, made him appear soft and genteel. Steve couldn't help but envy Sharon for the catch she was netting. If he could give Richfield points off for a fault, it would be that he was too sweet and needed a harder edge to him to make even harder decisions. But that was only because Steve wanted him to be cruel and sacrifice others for his own gain. Isn't that what business was all about? Capital gain? But this was not business, it was an affair of the heart. And that meant games. *Capital games.* Dangerous decisions that would make or break people's lives.

"...as you can see," Mark continued, "we need more web-based marketing. Your market appeal is world-wide, Mr. Foist. Why not open the boundaries and extend the advertising to a global market? Once the web-ads are in place, I suggest you show television promos in the Asian markets. Particularly Japan and especially China, the new powerhouse of world economy. By doing that, there is no limit to the consumer market." He paused, then asked, "What are your thoughts on going global?"

"I love the idea, Mark," Mr. Foist replied enthusiastically. "It had occurred to me previously, but I just never imagined Roland Matthews as the man to take my products into the future. To be honest, I considered looking elsewhere for an advertising agency, but I don't think that's necessary now."

Steve watched the smile broaden on Mark's face. The savior of Parsons & Company strikes again.

Mr. Foist turned to Steve and asked, "Was there anything you were going to add to the presentation?"

"No. I'm just eye candy," Steve joked, then when it wasn't understood in the way he had anticipated, he sat up and leaned over the table to the big man. "I'm here to tell you that if you need someone to promote your high quality products, you can count on Mark to do it. He's the latest asset to Parsons & Company, and I don't know of anyone more capable. As for my contributions, I'm the back-up for Mark. I'm the enforcer of the plans."

Mark quipped, "He's ex-LAPD, can't you tell?"

That amused Mr. Foist immensely. "I like it. I like the two of you. When can we get started?"

Mark instantly located copies of a new contract and handed them over.

As they were signed, Steve knew it meant millions to the company and a huge percentage for them as well.

After more details of which products were to be featured and how, Mark closed down the computer program as Steve gathered up the paperwork and placed it into Mark's briefcase.

"Well done, boys." Mr. Foist rose up along with his assistants and extended his hand.

Steve shook it, then Mark did as well. "Thank you, sir. I know you won't be disappointed."

Nodding and smiling as they left, Mark whispered, "Let's get the new ideas directly to the web designers. Have them put everything else on hold and work on this."

"I agree. I'll let Harold know and we'll do it today so they have the rest of the week to work on it." Steve opened the door for them and they walked out to the parking lot in the heat.

"They need a top notch website. Should we look outside the company?"

"No. Let's give our guys a shot first." Steve waited as Mark unlocked the doors of the TVR, then climbed in and rolled down the window in the warmth of the interior.

Mark started the engine and air-conditioning instantly, then made sure his computer and briefcase were set behind the seat securely. When he had finished and cool air was coming out of the vents, he reached out to Steve for a handshake. "Well done, partner."

Eying that hand with some reservation, Steve intended on a quick shake, then more glazed stares out of the window. When Mark used his middle finger to tickle Steve's palm, like he had done once to Mark, Steve turned quickly to face him. "Don't do that." He took back his hand.

"Steve, don't be like that." Mark leaned towards him inside the confines of the car.

As soon as Mark's hand rested on his thigh, Steve moved it off. "I said stop. Stop teasing me if you're not going to do anything about it."

"I don't want to stop." Mark placed his hand on Steve's broad thigh again.

Twisting away as far as he could in the tight compartment, Steve leaned against the passenger door and rubbed his face wearily. The night of hysterical crying over the situation washed over him painfully. He had to cut his losses. It was killing him. "Please just drive us back to the office."

"Steve…"

As Mark's hand rubbed his leg, moving to the inseam and close to his crotch, Steve stiffened and held his breath. "Mark! Stop tormenting me!"

"I'm not doing that!" Mark answered in the same urgent tone. "I'm caressing you."

His temper rising fast, Steve swiveled back around and snarled, "You call off the wedding yet?"

Mark's eyes blinked wide in surprise.

"Did you?" Steve repeated, more angrily. When nothing returned in reply, he shoved Mark's hand off his leg. "I didn't think so. Stop touching me. I'm beginning to feel like a fool who you are using as some fricken toy."

"What?!" Mark gasped. "That couldn't be further from the truth!"

"Oh, fuck you. Get me back to the office, will ya? I'm sick of stroking your ego."

"Steve, that's unfair…"

"Unfair?" Steve choked at the irony. "You want to know what's unfair? Getting me to fall madly in love with you and then marrying that idiot! That's what's unfair!"

Reaching for him as if to embrace him to comfort him, Mark attempted to touch him but Steve flinched back. "I am just as mad about you, love."

"Oh?" Steve asked sarcastically. "You love me and are marrying someone else? How inconvenient for you."

"No. It isn't like that. It's the impropriety, the duty—"

"The what?" Steve roared, "Duty? Oh, that's it. Either drive me back to the office now or I'll grab a cab." Steve reached for the door handle.

"No. No, I'll drive you. Stop." Mark grabbed him.

He never remembered being this angry or this hurt. Biting back his anguish, hating that he was right next to him and the hostility, like a wall, made it impossible to touch him, Steve needed time off. He couldn't see him every day right now. He needed to distance himself from him.

The minute they parked the car, Steve hopped out and hurried to the elevator without him. As Mark gathered up the paperwork and laptop, Steve rode the elevator alone and made his way to Mr. Parsons' office.

With one knuckle Steve rapped his door. "Ya got a minute, Harold?"

"Yes, Steve, come in. How did it go? Where's Richfield?"

"On his way with the paperwork. We signed a spectacular deal. You'll be very pleased, sir."

"Well done!" He reached out his hand.

"On that note, sir. I haven't taken time off for ages. Could I take a couple of weeks?"

"You've earned it, my boy! Anything else in the works we need to follow up on?"

"Not at the moment. I'm all caught up."

"Put in your request form and have a good vacation."

"Thanks, Harold. You have no idea how much I appreciate it."

Mark tucked the laptop under his arm as he pressed the elevator buttons. Even though he had just made himself very rich, he felt devastated. Finally coming through the door of his office, he set his things down, found the contracts, and then brought them to Mr. Parsons. He rapped on the door and then smiled weakly when asked to come in.

"Well done, Mark! Steve already told me about the deal. I'm very pleased."

"Thank you, sir. Here are the papers." Mark set them on his desk.

"The two of you make a hell of a team! A hell of a team!"

"Yes. Yes, sir."

"Do you need some time off?"

"Sir?" Mark tilted his head curiously.

"I was just wondering. Steve has asked for a few weeks off. I just wondered if you would as well."

"Oh. No. I already have some time booked in for next month."

"Yes, that's right. For your honeymoon. I forgot about that. Right. Well, go ahead and take the rest of the afternoon off. It was well deserved."

"If it's all the same to you, sir, I'll just stay and finish my day."

"Suit yourself. Well done again, my boy, well done!"

"Thanks." Mark walked down the corridor with a heavy heart. He peered into Steve's office but it was dark and silent. Scuffing his way to his own, he closed the door and dropped down on his chair, hiding his face in his hands.

Chapter Sixteen

Steve sat facing the setting golden sun. While his toes wiggled in the warm sand, his view was lost on the horizon and the crashing waves. The laughter of children and the shouts of their playing were lost on the stiff breeze blowing from the ocean. A dog shook off its fur, the water sprayed in a spiral pattern. Couples strolled hand in hand wearing bikinis and Wayfarers.

Leaning back on his forearms, Steve inhaled the fresh air and even behind his sunglasses he had to squint his eyes in the glare as seagulls glided by. When was the last time he took a break? He tried to remember. Oh yes…Sonja and he went to Hawaii together. It was bliss. Staring at the setting sun and surf in Kihei, a tall exotic fruit-filled cocktail in his hand and that beautiful woman's incredible dark skin shining in the warm night. He remembered them cuddled up together on the volcanic sand, her back pressed against his chest, smelling her perfume and loving the heat her body emitted as he wrapped his arms around her, keeping her warm.

Discreetly he wiped at a tear and then looked around to see if anyone was watching him.

Where and how did it go wrong?

His thoughts inevitably turned to Mark. Did he just make bad choices? Well, he didn't even know he was engaged when they made love in the desert. No, that information came much later, after he had taken his heart.

"Oh, Christ…" he moaned, lifted his glasses and wiped his eyes again, then noticed a woman staring at him and decided to leave the beach. It was cooling off and he wasn't dressed for the night air. Standing, brushing off his legs and feet from the sand, he slipped his loafers on when he reached the pavement, and raised his sunglasses to the top of his head.

A bookstore was among a small selection of stores across from the beach. The Uncut Buzzard. The name brought a slight smile to his lips. The aroma of fresh bread and coffee from the café on one side of it competed with the scent of incense and candles in the mystic shop on the other. When he opened the door a bell jingled. He scanned around curiously and noticed a good looking man in his forties with long hair in a ponytail smiling at him from behind the counter. Steve smiled back courteously, and then browsed the aisles. Horror, Westerns, Romances, Biographies, Health and Well Being; the topics were listed on the shelves in large letters. The words Gay & Lesbian caught his eye. He casually glimpsed around him to see if anyone was spying and then stood in front of it curiously. It was divided into non-fiction and novels. The non-fiction depressed him instantly, so he tilted sideways to read the jacket covers for an interesting title. *The Kiss* caught his eye. Reading the blurb on back he shook his head at the irony. It was a male love story about an American and a Brit. "How appropriate," he mumbled and looked to see how much it was.

"You'll like that one."

Steve startled at the comment and turned around to see the man from the counter smiling knowingly at him. "You read it?"

"Yeah. Great sex in it."

"Oh?" Steve smiled wryly.

"You ever read anything of hers?"

Steve checked the author. "No. Never heard of her."

"Check it out."

Nodding, Steve followed him to the cash register and removed his wallet. As he stood there and watched the man ring it up, Steve felt as if he had seen this individual somewhere before. Then it occurred to him where. "Aren't you Angel Loveday?"

A blush found the man's cheeks. "Yeah." He took Steve's money and gave him change.

"I love your old movies. I swear I've seen every one." Steve slipped the coins into his pocket.

"Thanks."

Taking the small bag with the novel in it, Steve looked behind him to make sure no one else was waiting to be served, then asked, "You still act at all?"

"No. I put that life behind me."

"Christ, you look fantastic. I have to admit, I had a slight crush on you."

"Did you?" he smiled, flattered.

"Yeah. I used to rent those videos all the time when I was on my own. You know." Steve winked.

"Yeah, I get it." He smiled shyly.

"Uh…you want to get a drink or something? You know, after you close up?"

Angel stared at Steve for a moment as if deciding if the invitation was one he wished to accept, then he checked his watch. "Hang on a minute."

Steve nodded and watched as he disappeared into a back room. A minute later a pretty blonde woman appeared and stood behind the counter. Overhearing his comments, Steve heard him say, "You're all right closing up, Summer?"

"Sure, Angel. Go ahead and enjoy yourself."

When she caught Steve's eye and smiled impishly at him, Steve blushed to the ears. Was it any wonder she was grinning? After all, Angel Loveday was the king of soft porn in the eighties. Everyone wanted a piece of him.

"What was your name?" Angel patted his back pocket, checking he had his wallet, then nodded for Steve to exit the shop first.

"Steve. Steve Miller." It felt oddly conspicuous to be seen with him suddenly, but Steve disregarded his doubts and they walked side by side to the nearest bar. Steve followed him to a table that seemed out of the main drinking area and against a wall in the dimly lit room. Once they had seated themselves and gotten comfortable, a waitress approached them.

"What do you have on tap?" Steve asked, setting his book package down on the table near a candle and some condiments. When she listed the selection he chose one and then heard Angel ask for the same. Watching her leave, Steve then gave his attention back to the attractive man across from him.

"What do you do?" Angel asked quietly.

"I sell advertising now. I used to be an LAPD cop."

"Wow, that's a big change. I can't imagine being gay in the police department. Is that why you left?"

"No. I didn't date guys at that time. I was still seeing women back then. Never mind. It sounds really stupid."

"No. Not really."

"What about you? Do you have a boyfriend?" When Angel smiled and averted his gaze, Steve whispered, "Sorry...I don't mean to pry."

"No. No, it's okay. It's a common perception that I'm gay, Steve."

In the moment of confusion that followed, the waitress set their beers down and asked if they wanted to order any food. Angel ordered them a plate of nachos to share and after she left he stared at Steve for his reaction.

Finally he said, "You're not gay?"

"No." Angel laughed softly.

"But...?"

"The movies...I know." Angel sipped his beer.

"You...you sucked guys' cocks."

"I did. But it was for the film. I'm not gay, Steve. Sorry. I didn't mean to lead you on or anything."

162

"No! No," Steve said quickly. "I'm not looking for an affair. No. I just needed some company. I took some time off to get my head straightened out. I'm here on my own for a few days. You know, just to unwind and think things through. The last thing I need is more complications."

"Oh. Good. I didn't know if—"

"No." Steve smiled at the odd mix-up. "It's funny. I used to be able to just ask a guy out for a drink years ago, and that's all it was. Booze. Welcome to the 21st century."

"Naa, welcome to California." Angel raised his beer bottle for a toast.

Steve tapped it with his then drank a sip. "Good. I'm relieved in a way. I just wanted someone to talk to. I've been sitting on the beach since early this morning and my thoughts are starting to depress me."

"I'm a good listener. What's going on?" The nachos were set down, along with guacamole and sour cream.

Steve waited as the waitress set out plates, silverware, and napkins, then left.

"Dig in." Angel took some chips onto his plate and ate them.

"How did you suck guys' cocks if you weren't gay?"

A sly smile played on Angel's lips. "You have any idea how many times I've been asked that?" Angel looked around first, then added, "All right. I am gay. I just don't want my son Oliver hearing about it. So, shhh." Angel winked.

"My lips are sealed, Angel. Don't worry. I'll bet the pay was incredible for the eighties."

"It was. I was rolling in it, then drank it all and snorted it up my nose. I'm older and wiser now. And I have a son to think about. But, I don't need to vent, you do."

Taking a moment to think, Steve then searched those glamorous light eyes of his and whispered, "Christ, Angel…I am really suffering over this guy I work with."

"Oh? He know you have a crush on him?"

"We made love. We went to some stupid retreat in the

163

desert and ended up lost. Screwed like bunnies all night. Then he turns cold and tells me he's engaged, then he comes to my place and lets me do nasty things to him, then he gets cool again and talks about duty…my head is screwed up so badly now, I don't know whether to kill him or kidnap him."

"Engaged, huh. That sucks." Angel flagged the waitress down for another round of beer.

"Yes. The wedding is supposed to be August fifteenth."

Angel checked his watch. "Less than two weeks away."

"I know. I'm sick about it. I'm so in love with him it's killing me."

"How does he feel about you?" Angel sat back as two more beers were set on the table.

Steve waited until she left, then set his empty beer aside and took the fresh one to his lips. Once he had sipped it, he replied, "I know he's crazy about me as well."

"Uh huh. Have you ever been married, Steve?"

Seeing his stern expression, Steve said, "No. I got close but we never tied the knot."

"Did you plan the wedding?"

"No. We broke up before we got engaged."

"Right. Well, let me tell you about weddings. They are like steamrollers. Once the planning begins, they are nearly impossible to stop."

"Are you defending him?" Steve dipped another chip into the green avocado goo.

"Yes and no. He may not want to get married now that he's met you, but try and stop a wedding in progress. Good luck."

"But…" Steve fought with himself to not get emotional. "But isn't it worse to go through with it and find out soon after what a mistake it was?"

"You'd think so. But most men would sooner divorce than call off a wedding."

"Shut up!" Steve exclaimed in disbelief.

"I am not kidding you." Angel ate another chip.

"So…you're saying once he gets this wedding over with, he'll divorce her?"

"I can't say that. I don't know the guy. But if he's in the closet and he thinks this wedding somehow will get the suspicion off his back then he may go through with it just to show that he is legitimately straight."

That sat Steve back. He cradled his pint of beer and thought long and hard about it.

Angel wiped his lip with a napkin, and said softly, "If you two really love each other…you don't know what he's thinking about doing. He may be planning on an annulment soon after."

"No. I don't believe he'd do that. He's really a decent guy and he'd really hurt this woman. You have no idea what he's like. I swear, Angel, he's the best looking fucker I've ever seen. Even prettier than you were in those movies. And damn! You were hot!"

"Were?" Angel joked, then shook his head teasingly. "Never mind."

"No. Seriously, Angel, you're still really good looking, but, Mark…well. I can't explain how gorgeous he is. And he's such a smart fucker. And the body on him…"

Angel smiled as Steve got lost. "That good, huh?"

"Believe me. If you met him, you'd suck *his* cock."

Angel roared with laughter.

Smiling adoringly at this icon of the wildly erotic Plimpton films, Steve whispered, "Too bad you're not gay." Steve winked wryly at him. "I'd love to say I shagged Angel Loveday."

"You know how many times I've heard that one as well?" Angel's eyes twinkled mischievously.

"Hundreds…" Steve leaned across the table to him, feeling the beer buzz finally.

"Hundreds." Angel winked.

Even though he was only an hour's drive away, Steve

had rented a room near the beach. It seemed important not to stay at home in case someone, namely Mark, tried to contact him. He had shut off his mobile phone and resisted the urge to check his messages.

After he and Angel parted company, Steve thought about everything they had said and he knew that even though he had never met Mark, Angel was dead right. Mark had lived with the stigma of being gay most of his life. Here was his chance to prove to everyone he wasn't. He'd become the husband, the family man, and all that murky mist about his sexuality would dissipate. It was as if Mark just didn't want to hear the chorus of *I told you so* from all those people who pointed their finger in suspicion and told him he was gay even before he had come to accept it himself.

The only problem was the painful truth. Mark was gay. Gay and in love with a man. What Steve wanted to know was how strong was he? Could Mark stand up to the fears and intimidation and be himself or would the pressure to conform win out? If Steve had to lay money on it, he'd say Mark would indeed marry Sharon and he and Mark would never touch again.

He clicked on a light that was on the nightstand as the sunlight vanished from the hotel room. Propping up the pillows, he opened the new novel to page one and began a long bout of reading.

Mark parked in front of Steve's house. He wasn't answering his phones, or returning his messages. Placing the car in park and shutting the engine, Mark walked up to the front door and rang the bell, then pounded the wood loudly. The house appeared vacant and dark. "Where the bloody hell did you go?" Mark shouted at the empty windows. Rubbing his face in frustration, he took his mobile phone out of his pocket and dialed Steve's cell phone number once again. When the service picked up he said, "Steve, I know you're getting these messages, please call me. I need to speak to you. Please." Pausing, thinking of something more to say, he just bit his lip angrily and disconnected. Hesitant to leave, knowing this was the only connection he had to Steve besides his empty office at work, which he was spending too much time in as it was, he leaned his back against the screen door and stared out at his car as it sat across the street. Then he slowly sank to the front stoop and sat down, his head in his hands, and tried to think.

The rehearsal dinner, the bachelor party, picking up the tickets for their honeymoon trip, more gatherings with both families, his London relatives coming in and staying with him—it was all beginning to overwhelm him and the panic that seized him in the night was like a heart attack. He couldn't sleep, couldn't eat, and drank himself forgetful every chance he'd got. With Steve away from the office, he made as many appointments as he could to not be there. What good was wandering around that place without Steve there to enjoy?

Every time he noticed a patrol car drive past him on the streets he thought of the night they had played cop and captive. Just the sight of that uniform put him into heat now. If he stopped one, would they know him? Could he chat about Steve with them? Perhaps they'd know where he'd likely to have gone on holiday? These were the absurd thoughts he had running in his head, and the pain of missing that man was becoming unendurable, just as the company of Sharon and Jack became intolerable. Question after question, they would pry. Accusing glances whenever he lost his concentration. The badgering was becoming so accusatory he was about to find a hotel to stay in just to get away from them both.

The wedding. A monster so enormous it had become a living, fire-breathing thing that was looming out of control. His mother, his step-sister and brother, her parents, her sister, her aunts, cousins, all descending on him like a plague. 'Aren't you excited?' 'She's a lovely girl.' 'When will you have children?' 'I'm so happy you are finally settling down.'

A scream welled up in his chest. It took everything he had not to voice it and alert the neighbors to a stranger sitting on the ex-cop's steps.

A car parked behind his TVR. A man stepped out of it and walked directly towards him, a very concerned look on his face.

Mark stood up and tried to appear normal in the awkwardness.

"Can I help you?" Barry asked warily.

"Uh. Sorry. I…uh…thought perhaps Steve would come home soon."

"He's away." Barry moved to the mailbox and took out the letters that were inside it. "You must be the British guy he works with."

Mark brightened. "He mentioned me to you?"

"Yes. I'm his brother-in-law. He told us you were getting married soon." Barry tucked the mail under his arm and stood back from him.

"Aye…" Mark nodded sadly. "You wouldn't happen to know where he is."

"I do. But, I'm not sure he'd want anyone to know."

"I do need to speak to him. It's urgent I find him."

Barry looked around the neighborhood as if the answer as to whether he should reveal the location was lurking in the bushes.

"Please. I know part of the reason he—no, let me be honest. The entire reason he has left for this break is because of me. Please. Tell me where he is. He's not returning my calls."

"I don't think I can. Like you said. He wanted to get away from all this to think."

"Please." Mark thought he would cry if this man didn't give him the information. He was about to get on his knees and beg him.

And as if Barry knew the enormity of the pain Mark was

feeling, he sighed and said, "All right, but if you tell him you heard it from me, I'll never hear the end of it. You better not say you did."

"No. No, I won't. I'll make something up. I promise. Is he out of the country?"

Barry stared at him strangely. "No. He's still in California."

"Is he?" Mark brightened up.

"He's just on the coast in a place near Santa Monica."

"Oh, that's brilliant. Brilliant!"

Barry narrowed his lips on the information, then gave in.

His sunglasses on his head, his paperback in his hand, Steve strolled briskly through the lobby intent on finishing his reading on the beach in the refreshing morning sea air.

A male model appeared to be posing near the glass front windows. His long hair was swept back from his face, his white muslin sleeveless shirt was thin enough to show off a slight trace of his nipples underneath and his black cotton shorts were tight on his narrow waist accenting his bronze thighs and long lean legs.

Freezing mid-stride, Steve blinked and tried to comprehend why he was there, and savor that lustful leer he was receiving from him.

Like a predatory cat, Mark approached. The large bulge in his shorts seemed to move from side to side with each step he took.

Instantly Steve's throat went dry and his cock went hard as a brick.

"I know you wanted to be on your own," Mark purred as he moved nearer, "but I've missed you so much, I ache, love."

Mute, Steve shook his head as if to say, *No. Go away. You're not supposed to be here.* But no sound emerged from his tight vocal cords.

Boldly, Mark sank his hand into Steve's front shorts'

169

pocket, removing that hotel key. Then with a slight wiggle to his hips, he walked to the elevator, dangling it from his fine fingers.

And like a puppy dog after a cuddle, Steve followed.

The key inserted, the door opened and pushed back, Mark strut into the dim interior and didn't turn on the light. The curtains had been pulled shut from a late morning sleep, and the bed was still unmade. Mark slipped the *Do Not Disturb* sign on the doorknob, then closed the door.

Standing still, slightly mind-numbed by the surprise of Mark's presence and his irresistible sexual aura, Steve stared at him as if he weren't really human, like he was just some ghost that had come to tease him.

With the practice of years of seduction, Mark flipped back his hair, and then slowly started to unbutton his shirt. Steve actually licked his lips from the craving. The shirt dropped and that magnificent set of pectoral muscles stood exposed. Next Mark's hands slid down that tight abdomen to his shorts. The button opened, then the zipper, revealing nothing underneath them but skin and pubic hair.

A moan escaped Steve's throat.

Mark gracefully stepped out of them, then dropped them on top of the shirt. With both of his hands, Mark gathered himself up, offering that fantastic male anatomy to Steve as he gaped in awe.

"Oh, holy Christ," Steve moaned, the book slipping from his numb hand to bounce on the carpeted floor. Without another thought or word, he rushed over to this vision and wrapped around him, inhaling him, tasting him, rubbing his hands all over his silky skin and into his thick head of hair. When their mouths met Steve felt as if he was hit by a lightning bolt. Forget him? He thought it would be possible to forget him? Who was he kidding?

And Mark, his head back, his expression as if he'd reached nirvana, opened like a rose petal in Steve's strong hands.

It was as if he'd been given a feast after starving and he

didn't know where to begin to satisfy his hunger. But it was that British mouth and tongue he was after at the moment. Swaying, kissing, swooning, Steve felt as if he couldn't catch his breath. Stepping backwards to the bed, Steve waltzed them closer until he felt the mattress hit the back of his legs, then he urged Mark down onto it.

Staring down at him as he fumbled with his own clothing, Steve found a soft sensuousness to everything about him, including that loving gaze. Tearing off his garments to get naked, Steve finally enveloped him, skin on skin. As he squirmed all over his large masculine form, he moaned and whimpered like a baby and Mark did the same underneath him. The urgency of his need grew and Steve thrust his hips against Mark's thighs, wishing he had a bottle of lubrication handy and upset he didn't.

As if Mark sensed his desperation, he shifted on the bed until his face was even with Steve's hips, then devoured him.

Steve opened his lips to gasp at the penetration into Mark's wet mouth, then spun into a delirious climax as that tongue drew circles and lines from the base to the tip of his cock. With a guttural grunt, Steve's eyes clamped shut and his body erupted like it was volcanic and spewing hot lava. As he recovered, Mark lapped at him leisurely, fondling his testicles and scrotum as if petting a kitten.

With his chest still rising and falling rapidly, Steve got to his knees and shoved Mark back on the bed, then dove down on him, giving as good as he got. With his back arched, his legs spread wide, Mark seemed to be on the verge. Steve pushed his finger into his anus and massaged him inside as well as out, then tasted the cum as it shot out of Mark's cock. His breathy gasps like music to his ears, Steve didn't want him to stop, and drew more and more out of him until the moans turned into whimpers of ecstasy.

Sated beyond his wildest dreams, Steve finally removed his mouth from that fantastic penis, and panted as he rested his face next to it on Mark's pelvis. As if they had both just run laps around a track, they gasped for oxygen and dripped with sweat. Once his respirations slowed to something less painful, Steve opened his eyes with a blink. Mark's cock was still rock hard as if it was made of a lovely blush colored marble. Slowly Steve raised his head to see his face. Mark's eyes were closed and his chest continued expanding with his deep, fast breathing. Smiling wickedly, Steve wrapped his fingers around that organ and just held it, like a stick shift on a sports car. He heard a soft laughter come from Mark's lips.

"You want more, copper?" Mark giggled wickedly.

"Oh, yes," Steve replied, "I don't want to stop."

"Then don't stop."

Sitting up to look down at his entire body, Steve admired it in complete pleasure, then whispered, "How long have you got?"

"As long as you want."

"Yeah?" Steve was very tempted to ask why? How did he get away from the two others who seemed to have a strangle hold on his life. But why ruin the moment?

"Yeah," Mark breathed seductively.

Steve moved his hand up and down slowly, feeling the length in his palm. Inching upwards on the bed, he curled around Mark from behind and rubbed his face into his hair and neck, closing his eyes and savoring him. "I love you. I love you so much I ache."

"I know, love. I feel the same."

Then, instead of another wild bout of sex, Steve broke down, hiding his tears in Mark's long locks.

"Shhh, baby...don't upset yourself." Mark tried to twist around to comfort him, but Steve didn't allow it, squeezing him so tightly he could barely breathe.

Feeling like the worst fool, Steve did everything he could to stop crying, but the pain in his chest was like someone had impaled it with an ice pick. Suddenly, as if coming to his senses, Steve released him and scrambled off the bed.

Immediately, Mark rolled over to look at him.

Wiping his eyes roughly, Steve said in a hoarse, far away voice, "Why did you come here?"

"Why?" Mark sat up, making a gesture as if it was obvious why.

"Just go away and leave me alone."

Anguish appeared on Mark's face. "Don't say things like that, love."

"What was this? One last fling before you tied the knot?" Steve wiped at the fresh tears quickly before they fell.

"What? No, don't do this. Please."

"How did you find out I was here? Who told you?" Anger started replacing the hurt.

"Why does it matter? What matters is that I am here. And we are together."

"Oh? For how long? An hour? Come on, Mark! I'm sick of this game!"

"But, I can't live without you! I was miserable when you left!"

"It's all about you then?" Steve crossed his arms over his chest. "Poor Mark. He's miserable without his sex toy?"

"Please stop this." Mark ran his hand through his hair tiredly.

"Are you still getting married on the fifteenth?" Steve demanded to know.

Mark didn't answer. He didn't even meet his eyes.

"Get the fuck out of here!" Steve roared. "I came here to get you out of my blood! Do you hear me? And what do you do? You show up and seduce me! I can't live this way! I'm not the kind of guy who can have casual sex and it means nothing to him, okay? I admit it. I'm like a woman, okay? I need security! I need trust! I need something I can depend on, something that's permanent! I can't live with these small handouts from a man who is about to commit himself to a fucking woman! Now get out before I throw you out of here naked and on your ass!" He was panting

173

once more, but this time it was from fury.

Rubbing his face in agony, Mark let a painful sob slip out of his teeth, then he rose off the bed and stiffly reached down for his things.

As he watched him dress, Steve could hear those chocking sobs as they continued increasing in intensity. *Great*, he thought, *this is killing us both*.

Once he was dressed, appearing uncharacteristically disheveled and worn, Mark tried to stand straight and look him in the eye. The minute he did he began crying in deep heaving wails. The sound of it broke Steve's heart, but he knew Mark held the key to pleasing them both. Still, it was agony not rushing to comfort him.

"Oh, baby, baby..." Mark seemed to weaken at the knees, the water rushing down his face.

Steve felt his body leaning towards him, craving giving him the reassurance he so desperately needed. But he held back, arms crossed over his bare chest.

As if waiting for that kindness to come, when it didn't, Mark seemed to cave in. He wiped at his face to rid the tears, then struggling to see through them he opened the door and left.

As the emptiness engulfed him in the void, Steve's nice tall posture deteriorated to a defeated slouch. He scuffed to the bathroom and turned on the shower to wash up.

Mark hurried through the lobby dreading someone would see his tears. He jogged to his car and climbed in, then covered his face and wept like he hadn't wept since he was a tiny lad. His heart was rent in two and he didn't know how much more of it he could take.

There seemed little point to staying at the hotel. Steve packed his things and finally checked his messages on his mobile phone. The number of messages Mark had left surprised him. After deleting them, he dialed Laura's number and stood looking around the small room to see if he had forgotten to pack anything.

"Hello?"

"Laura, it's me. Why did you tell Mark where I was?"

"I didn't. Barry did."

"Laura!" Steve shouted.

"I know! But, he found him pining for you at your house and felt sorry for him. I told him he made a mistake, but it was too late."

"All right, never mind. I'm coming home now, so don't worry about the mail for the rest of the week."

"Sorry, Stevie."

"Forget it." He sat on the bed and looked down at his suitcase.

"Did you guys figure anything out?"

"No. I don't really want to talk about it."

"Okay. Well, I'm here if you need me."

"Thanks. See ya." He hung up and made sure his phone was off, then picked up the suitcase and made his way down to the desk to check out.

Chapter Seventeen

Straightening his tie in the mirror, staring at his pale, drawn reflection, Steve didn't want to go to Roland's retirement party simply because he'd see Mark there. He still had scheduled three more vacation days to go and it seemed strange to attend an office function while off, but he was in town and felt obligated. Checking his hair in the mirror, running a brush through it again, he stood tall and nodded at his weary face. "Good enough."

There was a valet outside the restaurant. He gave the young man his keys and then entered the double doors and immediately found Kevin, Charlie, Bret and David, milling around, drinks in hand.

"Hey, Steve!" Kevin shouted in greeting. "We didn't know if you would show. We thought you were on vacation."

"I am. But I couldn't miss it for Roland's sake. Where is he?"

"I don't know. Somewhere in there." He nodded to a very crowded loud room.

"Where's the bar?" Steve looked down at the cocktail in his hand thirstily.

Laughing softly, Kevin tilted his head. "I'll show you," he said and led the way.

As he passed, Steve nodded hello to the rest of the gang and didn't see Mark anywhere. He didn't know if he was grateful or disappointed.

Just as he was given a cold beer, Mr. Parsons appeared, patting his back warmly. "Good of you to come, Steven. It means a lot to Roland."

"No problem, Harold."

"How are you enjoying the time off? Resting?"

"Yeah. It's been great. Just great." He wondered if he could tell he was lying.

"That's fine, Steve. You just rest up. It's a well earned break."

"Thanks, boss." Steve noticed someone trying to toast the guest of honor. Mr. Parsons walked away to join in the cheer.

The room was called to attention and a booming voice was trying to be heard over the noise.

Steve felt someone brush his arm. Charlie was standing next to him. "Where's Richfield?"

"How should I know?" Steve bristled.

"Aren't you guys attached at the hip? Or somewhere around there?"

"You never stop, do you, Charlie? Mark's getting married in a few days. When the hell will you give it a rest?"

"He's still going through with that?" Charlie laughed callously. "Christ, what a farce." After more cheering and some garbled toast from another drunk individual across the room, Charlie asked, "You in his wedding?"

"What?" Steve laughed sadly. "I'm not even invited, you dork."

"Oh. I suppose it wouldn't make sense to have you there."

As if Steve had taken all he could to take, he grabbed Charlie by the scruff of his neck and choked him as he sneered, "If I have to keep listening to this bullshit, I'll make sure you're delivering it through broken teeth."

"Hey! Hey! All right." Charlie laughed at the violent reaction. "You'll come clean some day, Steve. You're just not ready now. Maybe after Mark's away on his honeymoon."

Disgusted with the topic, Steve shoved him back and walked away, out of the crowd so he could breathe. As he stood alone, sipping his beer, he wondered why he had come. Mark wasn't here, so what was the point? Feeling as if he'd made enough of an appearance, Steve set his bottle down on a table and left.

Running late, rushing out of the door, Mark checked the directions to the restaurant and raced over the streets to get to it on time. Finally pulling his car up to the valet, he handed him the keys and dashed inside. Checking his suit and tie were neat and combing his fingers back through his hair, Mark looked around at all the inebriated smiling faces and felt the noise level and stuffy heat were already too much for him. Kevin nodded and waved by lifting his glass to him. Mark acknowledged his greeting but didn't approach him. When he felt someone bump into him, he found Charlie's drunken grin. "You lookin' for Miller?" he slurred.

"No. Why? Is he looking for me?"

"He left. When he saw you weren't here, he left."

Raising his eyebrow skeptically, Mark doubted very much Steve confided that information and decided that was all Charlie's assumption. "He's on holiday. I wouldn't think he'd want to spend too much time with work colleagues."

"Oh? Is that the excuse you want me to use?"

"Why don't you mind your own business, Charles?" Mark said coldly.

"And why don't you admit you two are lovers?"

Stiffening up in anger, Mark walked away from his intolerable presence to shake hands with Roland, then think of a reason to leave.

Steve parked in front of the wrought iron gates and sighed deeply. There was no way of knocking on that door now. Jack would nail him with one punch no doubt. In some sick way he craved a good fight.

Just before he put the car into drive after staring at the house for a half hour, a patrol car cruised by slowly, shining a light into his face. Steve covered his eyes from the glare and couldn't see a thing beyond the intense ring of white.

He heard the scrape of a shoe and then someone asked, "You have any reason to be parked out front here, sir?"

"Christ, shut off the stupid light, you're blinding me." Steve kept his arm up as a visor covering his face. The light was removed from his direct eye level. He blinked and read the name tag of the officer. "Jesus, Jessie, I haven't been gone that long. Don't you know who the hell I am?"

Jessie leaned closer to get a better look at Steve's face. "Miller? What the hell are you doin' out here this late? You know what it's like in this neighborhood. If anyone stops for more than a minute they call us."

"Yeah, I know. Sorry, Jes." Steve gestured to him to move away from his door. He stepped back, allowing Steve to climb out of his car.

Jessie shut off the spotlight and they stood together speaking quietly.

"What are you doin' now? I heard you were working for some advertising firm."

Folding his arms over his chest, Steve leaned back on his Mercedes and smiled. "I am. It's good money, but not nearly as exciting as working the street."

"Come on back. We can always use you." Jessie cocked his ear to his radio, and then told the dispatcher he was under control.

Steve heard his vehicle registration broadcast over the air, and shook his head at the irony.

"Ten-four," Jessie said into the mike, then gave Steve

back his attention. "You still with Sonja?"

"Naaa. She dumped me ages ago."

"No! I'm so sorry, bro. What happened?"

"I don't know. She just decided we didn't have enough in common or something." Steve shrugged helplessly.

"Oh, that's rough. After all you two went through. I'm sorry."

"Yeah. Tell me about it." Steve sighed, then said, "You shaved your head just like Sgt. Casey. I like it."

"It's easier than the damn afro. I think all the brothers are doin' it."

"Looks good on you."

"Thanks. So, what the hell are you doin' out here at this time of night?"

"Just seeing if a friend of mine was home. I suppose I sat too long waiting to see if his car would pull up."

"Oh. Right." He nodded, then listened to a call come out over radio.

"You need to get that?" Steve asked.

"I should."

"Go for it." Steve smiled.

"It was great seeing you again, Steve. We should go out for a beer."

"I'd love that. You have my number?" Steve found his wallet and handed him a business card.

"Oooh, Mr. Vice President of Media Operations... Sounds impressive."

"Here." Steve took the pen out of Jessie's chest pocket. "Let me give you my home number." He wrote it down, then handed him back the card and pen.

"Cool. I'll call you."

"How's Isaac doing?" Steve asked as Jessie walked back to the patrol car.

"Good. I'll tell him you were asking about him."

"Thanks. See ya." Steve waved and climbed back into his car as Jessie drove off. Sighing tiredly, Steve started the engine and left, thinking of a hot shower and a good night's rest.

Mark drove home in a very bad mood. His thoughts dark and frustrated, he blinked his eyes tiredly at a police patrol car cruising down his street, then hit the remote control button that opened his electric gate. Once inside his domain, he shut off the car engine and hoped Jack would give him some peace. He needed to just go to bed. He was too tired for another confrontation. All he craved was peace and quiet.

Chapter Eighteen

Though he wasn't due back until Monday, Steve stopped by the office the Friday to check to see if he had anything he needed to take care of over the weekend. In casual clothing, jeans and a black t-shirt, he nodded hello to the few employees who spotted him, and then found Mary at her desk.

"Hey, Mary."

"Mr. Miller! How was your time off?"

"Fine. Look, I just stopped by to check if there was anything urgent I needed to get to on Monday. I just wanted to be prepared."

"Yes. Yes, as a matter of fact..." she replied, and then looked through some of her notes.

As she thumbed through her paperwork, Steve looked over the dividers for any sign of Mark.

"Here. This is from RJ Foist. Mark asked that I specifically give it to you to handle while he's off."

Taking the paper from her, sinking at the reminder of Mark leaving for his honeymoon on Sunday, Steve read a message for him to continue to monitor the web designers for their completed design. He nodded.

"There may be one or two things for you on your desk as well."

"Okay, Mary. Thanks." He took the note with him and then passed Mark's office. It was dark and vacant. What were the odds he'd come in the day before his wedding?

A pile had accumulated on his desk. Sitting down to thumb through the stack, Steve tried to focus but couldn't do it.

"Hey!"

He peered up from his paperwork to Kevin's smiling face. "How was your time off?"

"Okay. How's it been going here, Kev?"

"Okay. A little quiet without you." He laughed.

"Yeah, no kidding." Steve laughed.

"Uh, you going to Mark's wedding tomorrow?"

"I wasn't invited." Steve tried not to sound too bitter.

"Oh. He invited the whole office to come. It's on the bulletin board, you know, the directions to the country club, etcetera."

"Is the ceremony in a church?"

"Huh? No. I don't think it had the name of a church on it. It's all going to take place at some fancy country club in Sherman Oaks."

"Oh..." Steve nodded, trying to smile but failing.

"If you go, see you there. There's bound to be plenty of good food and booze."

"Yes. Right." Steve waited until he left, then as if he was drawn to some scene of mass carnage, he walked to that dreaded bulletin board and looked for the note.

In a very elaborate scrolling print, the invitation for all to attend was hanging like a noose waiting for his neck at the gallows. The time, the place, the names of the involved "lovebirds" and the welcome to the happy event, was as if a fairy tale was about to begin. The bile came up in his throat.

Chapter Nineteen

August fifteenth had finally reared its ugly head. The night before Steve had drunk so much alcohol that he threw it up in the wee hours of the morning. He hadn't been that stupid or sick since high-school. Feeling sorry for himself and very hung over, Steve lay in bed and stared at the clock as it ticked loudly. Then, as if some magnetic force was urging him on, he managed to get out of bed and dressed. After he splashed his face, he stared at his unshaven jaw in dismay. His t-shirt was taut over his broad chest, and his shorts felt hot even in the air conditioned interior of the house. Like a pre-programmed robot, he locked the door to his home, then climbed into his car. It was as if he needed to see Mark go through with it to believe he had. It wouldn't matter if others told him about the wedding, the wonderful reception, or the food. He had to see this disaster for himself.

Mark felt sick. The tuxedo gripped him like a straight jacket. His hands were constantly cold and clammy and his insides were as icy as his nerves were shot. Jack kept touching his hair, as if making sure it was perfect. Mark couldn't remember the last time he had looked in the mirror. He hated himself and his reflection repulsed him.

"I have the ring," Jack said, holding it up to Mark's blind gaze. "Here's your boutonnière." He stuffed a white rose into Mark's lapel.

Mark didn't even feel him pin it on.

"I think that's everything." Jack stood back, looking at him. "You okay? It's normal to be nervous, Mark. Don't worry."

Revolted by the conversation, Mark's mouth formed a thin line. "I need a drink."

Spinning around, Jack noticed a few bottles on a rolling tray table and checked the labels. "Brandy?"

Mark nodded, reaching out his hand desperately.

Jack poured him a shot. Mark nudged him and indicated for him to double it.

Reluctantly, Jack poured more, then handed it to him. Mark shot it down in one gulp then waited for the kick. Instantly he handed the glass out for another.

"Maarrk…" Jack moaned.

Hitting Jack with the glass on his sleeve, Mark said, "Just pour the poxy booze, will you?"

Shaking his head, Jack refilled the glass. As he watched Mark suck it down and then shake his head from the after-burn, Jack said, "You sure you want to go through with this?"

"No!" Mark yelled, near hysteria, "I'm not bloody sure I want to go through with this!"

"Then don't! Mark, don't do it!"

"Don't?" Mark scoffed at the absurdity. "Don't go through with it after a year of planning? A three year engagement? Tens of thousands of dollars spent? Don't go through with it? Are you mad?"

"Mark! It's a commitment! A marriage! I'm just saying if you aren't one hundred percent sure—"

"One hundred percent sure?" Mark cried in anguish. "Jack, are you bleedin' insane? I'm not even one percent sure!"

"Oh, god, Mark…don't do it."

"More. More of that." Mark shoved the glass at him.

His face expressing his worry, Jack poured more. When

it wasn't quite enough for him, Mark snatched the bottle out of his hand and poured himself a generous glassful.

"Don't do this, Mark. Come on. Think of Sharon. You can't stagger out drunk."

"If I'm not drunk, I can't do it." Mark shot down the third glass.

A knock was heard at the door. Mark's mother poked her head in. "You ready, Mark? They started the music."

Already feeling the sensation of the alcohol on his completely empty stomach, Mark tried to stand tall, then nodded as if he were ready for that walk to the guillotine.

Steve couldn't get over the number of cars. A white stretch limousine was parked out front decorated with flowers and ribbons. A man in a tuxedo was parking cars and giving out bags of confetti. Avoiding the valet, Steve double parked, blocking someone in, but knew he'd be by far the first to leave.

"What am I doing here?" he sighed, sick to his stomach.

Drawn to the scene of the crime, Steve willed his shaking legs to move toward that reception hall. At his casual clothing and rough stubble on his jaw, someone stopped him at the entry.

"Sorry. I was running late," he explained. "I'm Steve Miller. I work with Mark at Parsons & Company."

The man nodded, his eyebrow raised at the lack of decorum, but Steve was allowed in. From the moment he entered the club house he could hear music. Forcing his legs to move towards the sound, he found himself standing in the back of a huge hall loaded with colorfully dressed guests, enormous floral bouquets, and white ribbons scalloped around the chairs. At the front stood Mark, Jack, and several other tuxedo clad males he had never met. Four bride's maids stood opposite them holding ribbon strewn clusters of white and yellow flowers.

It was as big as Mark had said it would be. Even from

where Steve stood he could see Mark's pale profile and nervous expression. The music changed in tempo and Steve had to step aside to avoid the bride and her father and mother walking down the aisle. He hid his face from her, twisting around, and moved to the farthest back corner of the huge room. Her long train followed her like a snake, moving soundlessly down the red carpet.

"Oh, god...oh, god..." Steve felt his eyes well up and the pain in his chest became unbearable.

She was coming down the aisle towards him. The veil obscured her face. He felt as if he were condemned to death. Somehow this nightmare wasn't reality. It was just that reoccurring dream he kept having over and over again. How did he let it get this far? As he looked around the congregation, he found her extended family standing to the right, his London relatives to the left, all anxious for the party afterwards. Jack's expression of worry hadn't changed for hours.

Should he feign a heart attack? He felt as if his knees couldn't sustain his weight anyway. It wouldn't be all an act. The alcohol was beginning to flow through his bloodstream with vengeance and collapsing seemed in order.

She was standing next to him now, a smile on her painted lips. Her father and mother had let her go, backing up to stand with the rest of the group behind him.

Oh, god...oh, god... Mark cried inside his head.

The justice of the peace said, "We are gathered here today to unite Mark Richfield and Sharon Tice in civil matrimony..."

Mark felt as if he lost consciousness. He really couldn't hear the man speak, only watched as his lips moved. He hoped someone would tell him if he needed to reply. A strange buzzing came to his ears. His body was trembling in waves he knew had to be visible.

Some rehearsed line came up and he wondered if he was supposed to say something. He nodded, repeating a line he couldn't remember a moment later. She said something similar. He lost interest and stared at the official's finger. He had a gold wedding ring on. "I do..." He wondered if he actually said that or just thought it.

Then somewhere in the back of his brain he heard his name.

"Maaarrrrk!"

It was distant and filled with pain.

"Maaaarrrrk!"

As if it finally hit his alcohol drenched gray cells, Mark turned around to look as did several other members of the wedding party. There, standing in the aisle by the back of the room, was the love of his life.

Steve was certain he was possessed. Something took over his body and mind, and he was unable to stop screaming Mark's name right in the middle of his wedding ceremony.

Mark heard someone say, "Christ, it's like a scene from *The Graduate*." Briefly he registered it was Charlie who had uttered it, laughing, "'bout time, Miller!"

Spinning around, Mark found Sharon's look of complete disbelief and then a strange mixture of shouts was heard around them. While some people were talking about removing the intruder, getting security, threats, others were whistling and cheering Steve on. Mark found Jack's face. To his amazement a very ironic smile was there, not anger, not jealousy, just irony.

"Maaarrrrk!" That pain-filled voice found his ears even over the growing volume of amazed comments around him. Seeing some of Sharon's family members about to run up the aisle and get violent with Steve, Mark finally decided to end the charade. He took two steps away from Sharon and towards his lover and cried out to him in desperation, "Steve!"

"I knew it!" Sharon threw down her bouquet and started ranting in that childish way that Mark detested.

Jack was trying to calm everyone down as the entire place seemed to dissolve into chaos.

With two rivers of tears streaming down his cheeks, Steve watched in complete awe as Mark made his way to him around several very confrontational relatives. He could hear the expletives as well as the cheering from where he stood and wondered how Mark was able to continue making progress towards him with all the battling going on between them. A few of the spectators began chanting Steve's name in support. Steve was trying to decipher what they were saying. Through his numbness he flinched at the noise, knowing he'd collapse in a fight he was so worn out, but as he listened harder he heard the people he worked with shouting, "Go! Go, Steve, go!"

"Steve!" Mark had to physically shove someone out of his path. The noise behind him echoed like a cacophony in the poor acoustics of the hall. Finally he stood in front of him, smiling sadly into his tear-stained, unshaven face. When they embraced Mark felt the most heartfelt relief he had felt in his lifetime. A roar of a cheer rang out from behind them from their co-workers.

With his arms around this man, Steve rocked him, crying at the feel of his body against his, the profound sensation that everything would be all right coursing through his veins. Once they had reassured each other, Mark twisted around to face a room full of very excited people. He raised his hands for some quiet, but it took a long while before anyone gave him the chance to talk. Behind him Steve was trying to stop crying, struggling to keep his emotions under control.

"Please!" Mark shouted, "Please... Let me speak!" Through the glares, scowls, and from the profane muttering of Sharon's family to the excited cheers of their friends, Mark finally got his moment. "I am truly sorry. Please forgive me. I know I should have stopped this wedding weeks ago, but I found I didn't have the courage to do it." A loud roar of protest mixed with cheers of applause followed. He held up his hands and begged for calm. "Please... Sharon, love, I am forever sorry. But you knew all along, love. You knew. Though I will apologize forever to you, I know in my heart this is the right thing to do. I'm so sorry. Forgive me. Forgive me."

The angry replies from Sharon and her parents were anything but forgiving. Steve grabbed Mark by the hand and urged him out of the room before people actually decided to get physical. One look at the growing unruly mob and Mark agreed. As they turned to escape the madness, Charlie and Kevin shouted, "We knew you guys couldn't stay away from each other! We knew it!"

Running with Mark out of the club and to the open-air parking lot, Steve made for his car and unlocked the doors. Mark climbed in and looked back as a few of the wedding party ran after him. "Hurry, love."

Steve started the engine and spun the tires to get out of the drive. In his side view mirror Mark could see shaking fists and rude gestures mixed between shouting cheers and thumbs up. With the skill of an experienced police officer, Steve nailed the accelerator and reveled in the engine's whine as he hit tarmac. A short squeal ripped the air as his tires gripped the pavement, then they flew over the open road eastbound.

Once they had a few miles behind them, Mark opened his stiff collar and pulled off his bow tie, tossing it on the floor of the Mercedes. Next was the rose on his lapel. He opened the window and tossed it out.

Watching him from the corner of his eye, Steve knew Mark's insides must be a scrambled mess from the nerves.

After he felt as if he had gotten as comfortable as he could, Mark reached for Steve's hand and held it tightly on his lap. "Where you headed, love?" he asked softly.

"Sante Fe. I know a great place in the desert we could stay."

A wry smile played across Mark's lips. "I do adore you."

"You too, hot stuff," Steve replied, bringing Mark's hand to his lips to kiss.

Grinning in pleasure, Steve found the signs for Interstate 40 and relaxed in the driver's seat as Mark caressed his leg gently.

Mark reclined in the seat and smiled to himself. "I guess we finally got what we wanted."

"Oh yes. I know exactly what I want."

"Naughty…naughty…"

Bursting out laughing, Steve felt his heart warm wonderfully and threw a kiss to the man next to him, who threw it back.

The End

About the Author:

Award-winning author G. A. Hauser was born in Fair Lawn, New Jersey, USA, and attended university in New York City. She moved to Seattle, Washington where she worked as a patrol officer with the Seattle Police Department. In early 2000 G.A. moved to Hertfordshire, England, where she began her writing in earnest and published her first book, *In the Shadow of Alexander*. Now a full-time writer in Ohio, G.A. has written dozens of novels, including several bestsellers of gay fiction. For more information on other books by G.A., visit the author at her official website at: www.authorga.com.

Also by G.A. Hauser:

Secrets and Misdemeanors

When having to hide your love is a crime…

After losing his wife to his best friend and former law partner, David Thornton couldn't imagine finding love again. With his divorce behind him, he wanted only to focus on his job and two children. But then something happened, making David realize that despite believing he had everything he needed, there was someone he desperately wanted—Lyle Wilson.

Young and determined, Lyle arrived in Los Angeles without a penny in his pocket. Before long, however, the sexy construction worker nailed a job remodeling the old office building that held the prestigious Thornton Law Firm. Little did Lyle realize when he gazed upon the handsome and successful David Thornton for the first time that a door would be opened that neither man could close.

Will the two men succumb to the tangled web of societal pressures placed before them, hiding who they are and whom they love? Or will they reveal the truth and set themselves free?

Naked Dragon

Police Officer Dave Harris has just been assigned to one of the worst serial murder cases in Seattle history: The Dragon is hunting young Asian men. In order to solve the crime it's going to take a bit more than good old-fashioned police work. It's going to take handsome FBI Agent Robbie Taylor.

Robbie is an experienced Federal Agent with psychic abilities that allow him to enter the minds of others. You can't hide your secrets and desires from someone that knows your every thought. Some think what Robbie has is a gift, others a skill, but when the mind you have to enter is that of a madman it can also be a curse.

As the corpses pile up and the tension mounts, so does the sexual attraction between the two men. Then a moment of passion leads to a secret affair. Will their love be the distraction that costs them the case and possibly even their lives? Or will the bond forged between them be the key to their survival?

The Kiss

Twenty-five year old actor Scott Epstein is no stranger to the modeling industry. He's done it himself between acting jobs. So when his sister, Claire, casts him in a chewing-gum commercial with the famous British model, Ian Sullivan, he doesn't ask any questions. He's a professional. He'll show up, hit his mark, say his lines, and collect his paycheck. Right?

Ian Sullivan is used to making heads turn. Stunningly handsome, he's accustomed to provocative photo shoots where sex sells everything from perfume to laundry soap. Ian was thrilled when Claire Epstein cast him in the new Minty gum commercial. He has to kiss his co-star on screen? No problem. Until he finds out Scott is the one he has to kiss!

Never before has a commercial featured two men, kissing on screen. Claire knows that the advertisement will be ground-breaking, and Scott knows that his sister needs his performance to be perfect. As the filming progresses and the media circus begins around the controversial advertisement, the chemistry between Ian and Scott heats up and the two men quite simply burn up the screen. Is it all an act? Or, have Ian and Scott entered into a clandestine affair that will lead them to love?

For Love and Money

Handsome Dr. Jason Philips, the heir to a vast fortune, had followed his heart and pursued his dream of becoming a physician. Ewan P. Gallagher had a different dream. Acting in local theater, the talented twenty-year-old was determined to be a famous success.

As fate would have it, Jason happened to be working in casualty one night when Ewan was admitted as a patient. Jason was more than flattered and surprisingly aroused by the younger man's obvious attraction to him. The two men entered into a steamy affair finding love, until their ambitions pulled them apart.

Now, one year later and stuck in a sham of a marriage that he entered into only to preserve his inheritance, Jason is filled with regret. Caught between obligation and freedom, duty and desire, Jason finds that he can no longer deny his passion. He plans to win Ewan, Hollywood's newest rising star, back!

A Question of Sex

Sharon Tice seems to have it all. She's beautiful, confident, sexy, and holds an executive position in her father's prestigious firm. But when her father puts her in charge of his latest building project, Sharon soon discovers that her life is missing something...Mark Antonious Richfield.

Mark is one of Los Angeles' most eligible bachelors, charming, charismatic and successful. His first encounter with Sharon takes him by complete surprise. The attraction between the two is undeniable and when they give in to the impulse to satisfy it, and one another, it's positively explosive.

After his first taste of Sharon, Mark is left wanting

more, and the sultry blonde is more than willing until she's introduced to Jack, Mark's roommate, and begins to suspect that they are lovers. Somewhere between rumor and innuendo lies the truth. Will Sharon put aside her fears and jealousy long enough to discover the possibility of love? Or, will it simply remain *A Question of Sex*?

This is a publication of
Linden Bay Romance
WWW.LINDENBAYROMANCE.COM

Recommended Read:

Metamorphose by J.J. Massa

Wanting them both was one thing, having them changed everything...

Built on a mystic-sensitive fault, the Porta branch of the International Worlds Museum is a busy place. Paranormal artifacts of all kinds can be found there, magic is a way of life, and citizens from other worlds come and go.

Wynn Ravensdale is the procurement agent for the International World Museum in the Department of Portable Antiquities and Treasure. The epitome of propriety, Wynn wants nothing more than to succeed at his job...except for perhaps Leena Keene and Rand Cooper.

Wynn's roommate Leena is beautiful, brilliant, and his twin sister's best friend. When Wynn's sister finds herself unexpectedly a single mother, it's Leena who steps in to care for the child. They were well on their way to fulfilling Wynn's fantasy of becoming a happy little family. Then the child's father, a blood drinker, showed up to reclaim what was his, leaving Wynn severely injured.

With Ellen and the child kidnapped and Wynn in the hospital, Rand Cooper offered help. Sexy Rand, may be rough around the edges, but his healing touch turned out to be just what Leena and Wynn needed. Together, will Rand, Leena, and Wynn find the strength, power, and love to rescue the missing and save themselves?

Printed in the United States
143139LV00004B/10/P

9 781602 020870